Explosive Reunion

LaMar County Justice Book 3

Dana R. Lynn

Contents

Verse

But they that wait upon the Lord shall renew their strength; they shall mount up with wings as eagles; they shall run, and not be weary; and they shall walk, and not faint.

—Isaiah 40:31

This book is dedicated to my children. You have inspired me to be a better person. Love you, always.

Chapter One

Sergeant Madalyn Blake tossed the remains of both her and her partner's lunches into the garbage can next to the coffee shop entrance and walked back to her cruiser. She shoved her hands into her coat pockets and held her arms stiff, keeping them close to her body to shield herself from the frigid March air. She ducked her head to avoid getting the icy rain on her face, but she couldn't do anything about the drops plopping into her hair. Thankfully, she'd taken the time to wind her hair into a bun at the base of her neck. Otherwise, it would be getting soaked right now.

Yuck. She should have worn a hat like she always told her six-year-old daughters to if they wanted to play outside on cold days. Now her little bit of hypocrisy was biting her back.

The moment she slid behind the steering wheel, she turned up the heat, released her hair from the bun and ran her fingers through the damp strands so they would dry. Then she slid her cheap sunglasses up her nose. Her partner, Sergeant Elaine Cardon, sent in the 10-8, notifying dispatch that their cruiser was back in service.

"That didn't feel like thirty minutes," Elaine grumbled, using the mirror on the back of the passenger side visor to fluff her short blonde hair before carefully reapplying her cherry red lipstick. She used a napkin to blot, smacked her lips, then looked around.

"Where do I put this?" She held up the lipstick-stained napkin.

"I just threw my garbage bag out."

Elaine shrugged and started to shove the soiled napkin into the door pocket.

Maddie cleared her throat and gave her a pointed look over the top of the sunglasses. If she let her, Elaine would leave her stuff all over the cruiser, and before she knew it, the inside of the car would look like the top of Elaine's desk at work. Maddie didn't care how Elaine kept her own spaces, but she needed some organization. She couldn't control everything, but the condition of her vehicle was one thing she could. And did.

"You saw me take our trash to the can. It's right over there." She waved a hand toward the front of the building. "Less than twenty feet away."

"Hold on." Elaine huffed and flung open her door. She stalked to the trash can and dropped the napkin in.

Maddie didn't roll her eyes, but it was a close call. Despite having worked together for nearly six months, she and Elaine had a cordial professional working relationship and nothing more. They had rubbed each other wrong since the day the petulant blonde had transferred to the LaMar Pond Police Department.

Maddie admitted to herself that she missed her former partner, Claire. But Claire had left so she could be closer to her husband, who worked out of a precinct in Ohio. It was only a couple of hours away, and she saw Claire socially every other month or so but still. Working with Claire or any of the other officers would have been less annoying. However, Elaine was a good cop, so she kept her opinions to herself. It didn't matter how much she liked the other woman as long as they worked well as a team and put criminals away.

That didn't mean Elaine didn't sometimes set her teeth on edge. But that was life.

Elaine flopped dramatically into her seat and closed the door with more force than necessary.

"Hey. No need to slam the door. We've not been called out or anything." Maddie sent a frown her way.

"I didn't slam it," Elaine said, a slight sneer on her red mouth.

Maddie bit the inside of her lip. It wasn't worth starting an argument. Besides, she suspected Elaine did it because she knew slamming doors irked Maddie. She had no idea why. No one did. What Maddie would never share with her partner, or anyone other than her former police chief, were the little things that triggered her PTSD, a lingering side effect of being married to a charismatic abuser.

Maddie was one of the lucky ones. The emotional abuse had been subtle for the first year of their marriage. When the physical abuse started two months after she gave birth to Piper and Paige, she'd packed her bags and filed for divorce the next day while he was at work. Then she'd moved back to LaMar Pond where she'd grown up. She had a feeling her old boss might have had a chat with her present chief, Paul Kennedy, but she'd never asked.

She'd lived in fear of her ex-husband coming after her and the girls. For nearly two years, she'd spent every day wondering if this was the day he'd find them. She'd kept their bags packed so she could leave at a moment's notice. She'd even scouted out several possible destinations for when they needed to move out.

The week before the twins' second birthday, she had gotten a venomous email from Alex's mother, Sarah, blaming her for causing his death. How she'd been at fault for his drinking and driving, she'd never figured out. The relief at learning they were finally free overwhelmed her. She'd blocked Sarah and moved on with her life.

The dispatch radio crackled to life. She let go of her memories—it did no good to dwell on them—and reached out to turn up the volume. For two seconds, white noise erupted from the speakers. Maddie winced.

"Ow," Elaine complained. "You're going to blow the speakers."

Maddie ignored her companion and focused on the dispatcher's voice. She knew him. Clyde Decker. Nice guy. He'd asked her out a few times. She'd been tempted to say yes but decided it wasn't worth the time to get to know him or any man better. She had the twins to think about.

"All units. Bomb threat. LaMar Pond Elementary School."

Her blood froze. "My kids are there."

"I'm responding." Elaine called in a 10-20, telling the dispatcher they were en route. "ETA: three minutes."

A lot could happen in three minutes. Too much. She'd seen it many times. Maddie forced herself to swallow the bile that rose in her throat. For a moment, she forgot how to breathe. She shook her head once to clear it. She'd break apart later, but right now her girls needed her to remain calm and in control.

"We're close, Maddie." Elaine said softly. "It's only a threat. It will probably be a prank. You know most of these calls are."

She nodded but didn't say anything. She flipped on the lights and siren and backed out of the parking space. When they arrived at the exit, she had to wait for a car to pass, despite the lights and siren.

"Come on. Come on." Her fingernails scraped the leather on the steering wheel. The moment the car passed, she pulled onto the street and made the familiar journey to the school. She didn't dare drive as fast as she wanted to due to the slick roads. Her thoughts flashed to her children.

Paige and Piper were first graders this year. They had been so scared when they found out they didn't have the same teacher. They'd always been in the same room all through preschool and kindergarten. They didn't know she'd specifically requested they not be placed together this year. Paige tended to dominate, and Piper had developed a bad habit of letting her older sister do all the talking.

Were her babies terrified right now? Or did they think this was just another practice drill?

Maddie shoved thoughts of her darlings aside so she could function. Doing her job well had never been so important. Her hands shook. She clenched them on the steering wheel. They were slick with sweat. She tightened her grip to still their trembling.

Pressing the gas pedal, she silently urged the vehicle to move faster. Traffic pulled over to the side, allowing the police cruiser to pass. Ahead of her, a single car remained in her way. She slowed. The speed limit was forty-five. The car couldn't have been going forty.

Maddie slammed the heel of her hand on the horn in two quick bursts. Finally, the car drifted to the side to allow her through.

Her phone rang. Elaine reached out and hit the button to answer the call. It was an automated message from the school district requesting she come get her kids. She'd have to call her mom.

"Elaine, can you dial my mom's number, please? I don't want to take my hands off the wheel to hit the call button."

"One second." Elaine selected her mom's phone number in the speed dial option.

"This number has a voicemail box that has not been set up."

Ugh. Her mom had just switched carriers and purchased a new phone. She'd have to remind her when she called back later.

It set her teeth on edge.

After what felt like an hour, they arrived at the school. Teachers and students were spilling out of the building, walking along the sidewalk. She recalled from the plan they'd sent home in the student handbook at the beginning of the year that the entire school would meet in the high school ballfield across the street. Parents and guardians were supposed to pick them up from there. Since the building was being evacuated, all students were being sent home. Pulling along the curb, she didn't even turn off the cruiser before jumping out and heading toward the building, her eyes scanning the classes. Both first grade teachers and their students were marching along the edge of the parking lot toward the sidewalk. Scanning the heads, she soon picked out Paige and Piper among their peers. Some of the anxiety leaked out, allowing her to breathe normally again.

Chief Kennedy stood with the fire chief. She made a quick detour in his direction, aware of Elaine at her side.

A couple of teachers cast astonished looks at her. Horror dawned in the eyes of a few. Apparently, not all had been informed that this was not a drill. Yes, this was real. It wasn't one of the monthly drills they were mandated to practice.

This was no practice. Someone had called in a credible threat, one that placed her daughters and all the children and staff inside LaMar Pond Elementary School at risk. Behind her, someone began to pray softly. Maddie nearly scoffed. She believed in God, but that was it. He hadn't saved her from brutality in the past. Why should she pray to someone who clearly didn't care for her?

"The bomb squad is on the way."

She nodded at the chief, her eyes making contact with Paige's fearful ones. When her daughter made a move as if she planned to run to her, Maddie lifted her hand.

Paige didn't like it, but she understood. Maddie had practiced just a scenario time after time with her girls. They were to remain with the adults in charge so she could do her job.

Within two minutes, the school had been evacuated. Children and staff stood shivering as the rain slashed down, coming harder every moment. The designated gathering area for the students and staff was across the street, a safe distance from the building. Most, including her twins, hadn't been able to grab coats or gloves before evacuating. Their clothes and hair were already soaked.

Parents began to arrive at the high school. She saw Nancy Dawns, the mother of a friend of the twins, walking swiftly along the sidewalk. She carried an oversized umbrella. Nancy lived down the block from the school.

"Chief, I'll be right back."

He raised his eyebrows but waved his agreement. She dashed across the street.

"Nancy!"

Nancy stopped, her arms wrapped around her little girl. "Maddie?"

"Hey." Maddie halted in front of her. "I can't get a hold of Mom. Could you…"

"Say no more. They can walk home with Chelsea and me. Your mom knows where I live. I'll wait for either you or her to pick them up."

"Great! I really appreciate it." She cleared it with the girls' teachers and gave both of her daughters a quick hug, explaining the plan before heading back to the school.

Hopefully, the bomb squad would arrive soon. If there truly was a bomb, they may only have minutes to defuse it before it exploded.

*

Sergeant Trevor Stone jumped up from his kitchen table when his radio went off.

"Bomb threat..."

Those two words sent adrenaline pulsing through his veins. He listened to the rest of the call, horrified. Who would hide a bomb at a school?

He'd be a few minutes behind the rest of the team, but he knew every pair of hands was needed in cases like this. *If he wasn't too late.*

Shaking the thought from his mind, he suited up and raced out to his truck. He wasn't officially working today, although he was on call. As a bomb technician and the only member on the team certified as a K-9 handler, he was an essential participant whenever an active bomb threat proved credible.

Whistling, he opened the door just as Misty, his two-year-old German Shepherd raced around the corner. Efficiently, he put her work vest on her, letting her know she was on the job. He gave her a command, and she hopped up into the front seat, settling herself on the passenger side in working posture. He smiled briefly at the sight of her sitting up at attention, then he swung up into the cab behind the wheel.

Trevor pulled out of the driveway and headed toward the school. His fingers drummed on the steering wheel. Two minutes into the drive, the first raindrops plopped onto the windshield. As the tempo of the rain increased, his fingers wrapped around the wheel. He shifted so he was sitting more erect in the leather seat. The combination of the pouring rain and wind buffeting the car made driving hazardous. The trees swayed as the storm beat down upon them.

There'd be branches down soon. He lightly tapped the gas, urging the truck five miles an hour faster. Any more than that and he'd be likely to hydroplane. That wouldn't help anyone. He had to balance the need for speed with safety.

Directly ahead of him, a large branch brimming with smaller branches covered with green leaves crashed onto the two-lane highway, effectively blocking his lane. He swerved the truck. The leaves scraped against the passenger side. Had there been oncoming traffic, he would have slammed into the obstruction. A lot of vehicles traveled this road daily. Punching the phone button on his dashboard, he called in the fallen limb. No doubt, there would be many such calls throughout the day.

He reached the school and parked his truck directly behind Lieutenant Marshall's vehicle. Lieutenant Marshall was the commander of the bomb squad. Although the members of his team were still a part of the LaMar Pond Police Department and trained with them sixteen hours each month, they were responsible for calls throughout LaMar County.

Giving Misty a quiet order, he led her over to where his team was already suited up and assembled. He strode over to them, noting his commander had already set a perimeter around the school exit to contain the danger.

Glancing at the building, he noted that besides the LaMar Pond Police Department, three different local fire departments had responded, including trucks from two different volunteer departments and two trucks from the Meadville fire department. Two ambulances waited on stand-by.

"You want me to take Misty through, boss?"

Marshall nodded. "Yes."

He looked to his faithful canine friend. She was ready to go, just waiting for him to give her a command. He led her over to the front entrance of the school, ignoring the feeling of hundreds of eyes aimed squarely on him and his K-9.

"Misty. Search!"

She wagged her tail once, then began to work. The other technicians and bomb squad members stayed out of her way. He followed her into the school. Misty's toenails and the scuffing of his shoes on the tiled floors echoed in the too-quiet building. It was like a tomb.

Misty completed the search of the first hall and headed down the next one. In the next hall, he heard a second K-9. They must have requested backup. He'd never complain. The more K-9s on the job, the less the chance a bomb would detonate and kill someone.

Sweat formed around his collar. Every second brought them closer to possible disaster.

By the time they ran into the second dog and his handler back at the main entrance, it was clear that there was no bomb in the building.

"We're clear," he radioed to his chief. "No explosives inside the school."

He stepped outside, intent on reporting to his commander, when a familiar face caught his attention. He'd know that halo of blazing dark red hair anywhere. Of course she'd be here. He lifted his hand and gave Maddie a casual wave, pretending his heartbeat wasn't tripping crazily inside his chest. She nodded regally, her hazel eyes remote. She looked like she was frozen from the inside out, and he didn't mean in reference to the weather, either. It took him a second, then he recalled what this alarm would mean to her.

His eyes widened. "Your kids?" he mouthed.

The corners of her mouth curled up in the barest hint of a smile. Good, they were fine. But this would haunt her, even though it was a false alarm. She'd never forget how truly vulnerable they could be.

The other handler, Sydney, followed his gaze. "You and Maddie a thing?"

He winced. Maddie would not appreciate it if her name was linked with his, or anyone else's, romantically.

"No. Just friends." It wasn't exactly true. Maybe they'd been friends once. But that was long ago.

He'd known Madalyn Blake most of his life. Lived on the same street for twelve years, in fact. She'd married a while back, taken the name Grant and moved away. When she'd returned to the area, she had twin girls, no ring on her left hand and had reverted back to her maiden name. She'd also adopted a guarded attitude around the men she worked with. Trevor had some suspicions about what had happened, but she'd never shared.

It had bothered him. After all, they'd known each other forever.

She'd also been Trevor's best friend until she'd married. Then without warning, their friendship had been severed. It was as if he'd been nothing to her. He recalled how she had supported him when his girlfriend had died from a prescription drug overdose when they were nineteen. He'd been shocked by the death. Was it an accidental overdose? That's what the coroner had ruled. Still, some small part of him wondered if Angie had known what she was doing. She'd been struggling to deal with her parents' divorce.

He'd never know the truth.

Maddie had been there with him through the worst of it. She was the only one who ever saw him cry over Angie. The only one he'd shared his deepest thoughts with.

The Maddie he had known then hadn't looked through him with eyes like ice.

His commander called him over. Shaking Madalyn Blake from his brain, he and Misty walked to Commander Marshall and reported their findings. His eyes wandered slightly while Sydney gave her report. Maddie had her phone out and appeared frazzled.

He almost snorted at the inane thought. Of course she was frazzled. There'd been a bomb threat at her kids' school. The fire departments began to clear up their emergency gear. One of the trucks began pulling out, momentarily blocking his view of her.

Sergeant Cardon joined Maddie, and the two of them held a brief conversation before ambling toward Chief Kennedy.

They walked past an old rusty car, and he heard a loud click.

Misty and the other K-9 both began barking, lunging on their leashes toward the sound.

"Maddie! Elaine! Run!"

Too late.

The car they'd strolled past two seconds ago exploded.

Chapter Two

A wall of heat forced Trevor to his knees. Metal, glass and ash dropped from the sky and fell on the other vehicles and the ground as well as the uniforms of the combined emergency personnel. Thick black smoke rolled off the engulfed vehicle. His eyes stung and watered. Rain continued to fall, splashing on the fire. The blaze hissed with each drop. A fire truck that had started to pull out of the school parking lot slammed to a halt, and the volunteer firefighters scrambled out.

The fire chief and the police chief were both shouting commands as officers and firefighters frantically grabbed gear to combat the inferno.

Where are Maddie and Elaine? Frantically, Trevor searched the area where he had last seen them. There. His gaze zeroed in on two bodies sprawled on the cold, wet blacktop where moments ago students had stood. He swallowed. The students. Thank God they were all gone.

"Sergeant Stone, stand down!"

Trevor jerked to a halt, his gaze flying to meet Lieutenant Marshall's. He hadn't even realized that he was moving towards the women.

"We need to make sure the scene is safe before we do anything."

Trevor grimaced. Of course, he knew this. For a moment, he had completely forgotten about protocol as his mind focused on his former best friend. He nodded at his commander, but it went against every instinct in his soul to leave those two brave women where they were. The firefighters went into action trying to contain the fire.

Trevor needed something to do.

"Sir! Permission to use Misty to search for other explosives in the cars parked here."

The lieutenant nodded. "Granted. But keep away from the fire."

"Bandit and I'll start in the lower lot." Sydney waved her hand towards the far side.

Trevor nodded. "Come on, girl."

Ignoring the camera crew from the local news station, he and Misty jogged over to the opposite end so she could begin sniffing out any other explosives. It took all of his self-control not to focus on Maddie. The best way to help her and all the others was to make sure no other bombs exploded. Until then, he had to assume everyone was at risk.

Still, he knew the moment the paramedics got the all-clear because he saw them racing to where the two women were lying on the ground. Gritting his teeth, he kept working.

"At least the bomb was planted away from the rest of the vehicles," one of the firefighters shouted.

Trevor shuddered once. That would have been a disaster. That one explosion could have set a chain reaction of blasts if other vehicles had caught fire and their gas tanks had ignited.

A chilling thought struck. Who were the targets? While the explosion happened after the children had all left the premises, had the timing been different, students and teachers would have been standing within two feet of the blast site.

Had the person responsible for this horrendous crime intended for it to be even worse? Had he or she planted the explosives with hopes of taking out the kids?

Misty returned to him. She'd found no other explosives. He glanced over at Sydney. She was tackling the final few cars. So far, they were in the clear.

Between the rain, the ash and the hoses spitting foam on what had once been a car, soon all of the emergency workers were covered. Still, they worked without complaining.

"On three."

Trevor glanced toward Maddie and Elaine. The paramedics had Elaine on a stretcher and we're rolling her towards the first ambulance. He blanched. From where he stood, she appeared dead or nearly there.

He whispered a quick prayer in his mind, barely aware of the words. Then, half fearful of what he would find, he rotated his head so he had Maddie in view. She was on her side, coughing and retching.

Relief flooded him. She was alive. Blood ran down her cheek from a nasty gash on her forehead, and there were holes in her uniform jacket where the flames had scorched it, but her eyes were open.

A reporter jogged toward him, waving a cameraman to follow her. Trevor glared at the woman. She stopped and turned to find another target.

Satisfied, he pivoted to see Maddie watching him.

"My girls," she choked out.

He moved closer and gave Misty the command to stay. The dog obeyed instantly. Trevor dropped to his knees beside Maddie.

"Maddie, they're safe. All the students left. They were sent home. None of them were injured."

She frowned up at him. "It's fuzzy. I recall asking Nancy to bring them home. What happened after that?"

The paramedic made a motion to hurry him up. He lifted a finger and nodded. "You and Elaine started to walk to Chief Kennedy. He was giving instructions. A car exploded."

She lifted her horror-struck eyes to his face. "I don't remember the car exploding. Where's Elaine?"

He wouldn't lie to her. "She's already in an ambulance. It's pulling out now. I don't know her condition, but she didn't look conscious."

She paled and searched his expression. "You'd never lie to me," she whispered. "Others might, but I know you too well. You would never tell me a lie to spare my feelings. Were there any other bombs?"

He saw Sydney and Bandit strolling back towards Lieutenant Marshall. He shook his head. "We looked."

"We have to get her on the ambulance."

Trevor stood and backed out of the way to allow the paramedics to work. They lifted her onto a gurney. Maddie bit off a groan. Trevor winced in response.

When they began to wheel her to the ambulance, he followed.

"Trevor."

He ran to the side of the gurney. "I'm here."

"What was his plan, Trevor?" she whispered. "Did he target the students? Or was this a bad prank?"

"We don't know yet." He shook his head, frustrated. He hated not having the answers. "Right now, we have very little information. As soon as we can, we'll examine the vehicle. See if there are any clues. You know no one is going to stop looking until we find out who did this, right?"

She started to nod, then winced. "Ow."

The paramedics loaded her onto the ambulance.

"Trevor!"

"What?"

"Call my mom. I've tried. Have her get the girls from Nancy Dawns' house."

"I'll do it, Maddie. I promise."

He stood back. One of the paramedics climbed in with Maddie and shut the door, blocking her from his view. The other got in behind the wheel. The siren blipped twice, letting those standing around know they were on the move.

Trevor deliberately turned his back and yanked out his phone. Maddie's mom was still in his contacts. Maddie never asked favors, not from anyone. But she'd asked him, and he wouldn't let her down. He'd told her he'd take care of her daughters, and Trevor never broke a promise.

"Hello?" A quavering voice picked up on the first ring.

Trevor knew Amanda Blake well. She had recently turned seventy-eight, and thirty-four-year-old Maddie was her only surviving child. She'd suffered the loss of her husband and her son years ago. Despite her age, Amanda was strong and sharp as a tack. That trembling whisper had nothing to do with her age.

She must have heard the news and knew her child and grandchildren were in peril.

"Mrs. Blake, it's Trevor Stone here."

"Trevor!" His name came out on a wail. "I missed Maddie's calls. And there was a call from the school. I turned on the news, and I saw my daughter on the ground. She was hurt."

"Yes, ma'am." He kept his voice steady. "It doesn't look bad. She talked with me before she went to the hospital."

"My granddaughters?" Amanda's voice had gained strength.

"Both fine. Mrs. Blake, Maddie asked me to call you. A friend of hers—Nancy Dawns—took the girls home with her. Maddie wanted you to go there and pick them up."

"Absolutely." Keys jangled on the other end. "They can have a long weekend with me. We'll bake cookies, and I'll teach them to crochet.

Piper's been asking. You tell Maddie she can count on me for whatever she needs."

He smiled. "She knows it. But I'll tell her." He started to hang up. Hearing her calling his name, he brought the phone back up to his ear. "I'm still here."

"Watch out for Maddie, please. And keep me informed of her condition."

He had no problem with her request as he intended to keep an eye on her. This whole situation bugged him, but he had the feeling he was missing something.

"Will do."

"Thanks Trevor."

He disconnected the call. Then he went back to work. He wouldn't rest until the person who'd planted the bomb and set out to kill someone was behind bars.

*

Maddie had never ridden in an ambulance before. It was not an experience she was anxious to repeat. She fought against the instinct to sit up and place herself at eye level with the paramedic who'd climbed into the back with her. Not that she had any issues with the female paramedic. Far from it. The young woman had proved herself to be both competent and compassionate. She and Sydney had met a few times, but had never done more than exchange a few words.

No, the real issue was that lying down while someone else sat up made you vulnerable. She'd been vulnerable before. Never again would she put herself in a position where someone else had that much control over her life.

But that wasn't the only reason she despised her current position. The vehicle bumped and shook. She bit the inside of her cheeks to keep a groan in. The driver must have hit a pothole. Again. He'd hit at least twenty so far. She'd stopped counting.

"We're almost there," the paramedic sitting next to her murmured.

"Is he trying to hit all the bumps?"

The other woman smirked. "Nah. But we are moving fast, and it's hard to miss them all."

All? Maddie didn't think he'd missed any.

She sighed. Her real complaint wasn't the driver. It was an excuse to keep her mind off her daughters. Had Trevor gotten ahold of her mom?

Come on Maddie. You know he said he'd call her. Trevor was as steady as they come. If he said he'd call, he'd call. It didn't help. Thank goodness the girls hadn't been left in school. She'd never have any peace if they had.

Although, if the school hadn't sent everyone home, she would have asked her mom to take them out. Once she answered her phone, that is. She was on the list of people allowed to remove the girls from school. Actually, when she'd filled out the paperwork at the beginning of the school year, Maddie had listed her mom and Nancy as the only people, other than herself, allowed to pick the twins up from school.

Certainly not her ex-mother-in-law. Or Alex's snotty younger sister, Danielle. Both of whom had let Maddie know she wasn't good enough for Alex the moment they'd met her. To this day, she couldn't believe she'd married him knowing what his family was like. Surely, seeing his interactions with them should have raised some red flags.

Nope. She'd been in love and so sure he was the one. Then he'd started to come between her and her mother and friends. It had been so subtle at first, she didn't realize how isolated she had become.

The only reason she'd bowed to the pressure and stopped working when she had was due to complications in her pregnancy. In hindsight, she knew that had she stayed with him and had he lived, he would have pressured her to give up the job she loved for good.

"Your heartbeat is spiking. Are you in pain?"

Maddie drew in a deep breath, forcing herself to calm. She was fine. Alex was dead. She had kicked his family to the curb, and they no longer had any say in her life. Even when her mother-in-law had threatened to sue for custody of the twins, the documentation from Maddie's doctor proving her claims of abuse had ended that campaign. They can't touch us. Not anymore.

Finally, the ambulance arrived at the hospital. Maddie hadn't thought they'd ever make it. She didn't know how much longer she could have remained lying on a gurney wondering what was going on around her.

The driver whistled as he exited the front seat. He slammed the driver's side door closed. The vehicle vibrated. A few seconds later, she heard him at the back door. She had to wait for the doors to be opened and for the gurney to be lowered before she was wheeled into the emergency room.

Her cheeks colored as people looked down on her when the paramedics pushed her past. She wasn't hurt that bad. She didn't even think she had a concussion. There was no reason she couldn't walk in under her own power. Even a wheelchair would have been an improvement. After all, her head no longer hurt, the bleeding had stopped, and her vision was fine.

Once again, it all came down to being vulnerable. She set her jaw and forced herself to let it go. The sooner they got her into the hospital and checked her out, the faster she'd be with her daughters. Nothing mattered except that.

She clamped her lips shut tightly and closed her eyes to deal with the sensation of moving. She was feeling a bit seasick from the motion of the ambulance combined with watching the ceiling tiles flash by. The odor of antiseptic assaulted her nose. *Ugh.* She hated the smell of hospitals.

They steered her into a small cubicle in the emergency room. She opened her eyes, glad that the motion had stopped.

"We need to transfer her to the bed," a nurse said, pushing into the small space behind them. "Can she move on her own?"

"Of course, I can. I'm not hurt that badly." This would be the real test.

She failed it.

She sat up too fast. Her head swam, and her stomach dropped. White noise filled her mind. When she could see again, she was flat on her back on the narrow bed, and the nurse was frowning down at her.

"That didn't go well. I want you to remain lying down until the doctor arrives."

She whisked out of the room, leaving Maddie alone. Sighing, Maddie tried to ignore the hustle and bustle happening outside her cubicle. Nothing was louder than a busy emergency room. The air sang with a cacophony of noises all meshed together. Machines beeping. Doctors, nurses and patients talking. A baby wailed, and someone else cried out in pain every few seconds.

There was nothing to do but wait. Maddie had never been especially patient. What if the doctor decided she needed to be held for observation? She'd go out of her mind if she was stuck in a hospital overnight after seeing the bomb squad, the police and emergency crews tromping up and down all around her daughters' school. She'd never forget that.

How could she ever send her girls back knowing how easy it had been for someone to plant a vehicle explosive? In her head, she went over every second of the morning while she waited for the emergency room doctor to make an appearance.

If the perp was someone playing games to scare people, would they have called in the threat? What was the point of getting all those kids out of school?

The acid in her gut curdled. Maddie rubbed her hand over her stomach, trying to control the nausea creeping around inside her.

A few minutes later, the doctor made an appearance. Finally. She was ready to crawl out of her skin, she'd been waiting so long. He asked her the typical questions as he examined her.

"How's your vision? Any double vision or blurriness?" He flashed a light in her eyes.

"Nope."

"What about dizziness? Nausea?"

"I threw up when I regained consciousness at the school, but haven't since then. And I was dizzy when I sat up too fast, but I'm not dizzy anymore." She deliberately didn't mention the way her stomach roiled, knowing it was due to her fear for her children. Only when she saw them would she be able to finally relax.

"Any headache?"

She shook her head.

He seemed satisfied and put his light away. "Well, the good thing is that you don't appear to have a concussion. I do want you to take it easy the next forty-eight hours or so. Any headaches or vision problems, call your doctor immediately."

"Yes, sir."

He glanced down at his tablet. "You have some bruising, and I suspect that your left wrist is sprained."

Although she didn't remember falling to the ground, her wrist had been hurting since she regained consciousness. She had fallen on her side and probably landed on it. At least it wasn't broken.

"When can I go home?"

The doctor peered at her over his glasses, reminding her of a former college professor who'd intimidated the entire class. "You can leave as soon as I release you. I am going to prescribe a brace for your wrist and some pain medication."

She wouldn't take the meds. She knew from experience most of the narcotics they prescribed would make her less aware of her surroundings. Maddie had decided long ago she'd deal with pain any day rather than lose her ability to function clearly.

"Thanks. The brace will help."

The corners of his lips lifted. She had the feeling he'd read her passive resistance perfectly. "Just come back if you have any trouble."

"I will."

He gave her another look then sighed. "The nurse will be in with your papers soon."

Soon ended up being another twenty minutes. She was ready to walk out without them when the nurse entered the cubicle. She waited while the nurse read through the document and went over the prescriptions and any side effects she might experience. Maddie nodded, knowing she wouldn't even fill the pain medication script. Her fingers itched to grab the orders and leave, but Maddie ignored the urge. The woman was doing her job. It wasn't her fault Maddie had trouble standing still.

Within minutes, she had cleaned up in the bathroom, making herself as presentable as possible, She walked out of the ER. She took her phone from her back pocket. She didn't know how, but it hadn't been damaged by the explosion or her fall. If she'd been thinking, she'd have called her mom while she was waiting. She blamed her slow thinking on the events of the day. Maybe her mom could come get her since her cruiser remained at the school.

"Maddie."

She spun at the familiar voice. "Trevor!"

Any desire to smile fled when she caught the intensity of his expression.

"What's wrong?"

He sighed, and she braced herself. Whatever he had to say, it wouldn't be good. Suddenly, every worry she'd had since the call came in after lunch surged to the front of her brain.

"My daughters!"

Chapter Three

Trevor caught the edge of panic tinging her voice. He held his hands out in a calming gesture. "Paige and Piper are fine. I got in touch with Amanda. She picked them up while we were still at scene. Text her. I'm sure she'll tell you all is well."

She whipped her phone in front of her and began tapping out a message, her fingers flying. Then she hit send and stared at the screen. The heel of her boot rapped on the floor as her leg bounced up and down. He recalled that mannerism from their childhood. Maddie always had trouble standing still. She was constantly fidgeting no matter where they were. In class, on the bus, in church. It didn't matter. Her lips moved while she waited. He could almost hear her begging her mom to text back.

Fifteen seconds later, her phone dinged. She looked at the text. The tension rolled off her like a wave receding from the shore. She let go of a long breath and held her phone out for him to see.

Piper and Paige grinned up at him, their hands covered with flour.

"She said they'd bake cookies," he told Maddie, laughing softly. "Looks like they're enjoying their time with Grandma."

She gave a small hiccupping laugh. Images of other times he'd seen her laugh like that flooded his mind. He pushed them aside. He couldn't afford to let past emotions distract him. If he wasn't careful, he'd forget that they weren't friends anymore. "They always have fun with my mom. She spoils them."

"Hey. That's what grandmas are for. They'll be fine."

She nodded and closed her eyes for a moment, inhaling deeply, then slowly exhaling. Her body stilled. Finally, her lids opened, and her hazel gaze rose to meet his. She was so strong and competent. Trevor often forgot she was several inches shorter than him. Not that she was short. Maddie was average height for a woman.

When she looked at him, instead of Maddie the concerned mom, he saw Sergeant Madalyn Blake. She'd be all right. He also knew she wouldn't stop until the person who'd done this heinous act paid for their crime.

"Officers!" a young nurse hurried to interrupt them before they could talk. They turned in unison. She stopped so fast she swayed and nearly bumped into Maddie. "Oops! Sorry. I know better than to rush like that."

"No problem. How can we help you?" He smiled to put her at ease. She didn't seem old enough to be a nurse. Maybe a college student in training, he'd guess.

"Oh! Right." She pushed a lock of hair behind her ear. "That other cop who came in? The blonde? She's awake and asking for her partner, Maddie."

"That's me."

"Good. I hoped you were. If you'd follow me."

They shrugged at each other and agreed. As much as he hated delaying telling her what they'd found, seeing to Elaine was just as important. She'd seen the car up close.

The young nurse ushered them into a room in the intensive care unit. "Please only stay for five minutes. She needs to rest but insisted that she needed to talk with you."

So warned, they entered. Maddie sucked in a breath. Trevor followed her. Even with her reaction, shock punched him in the gut.

Every time he'd seen Sergeant Elaine Cardon, every aspect of her appearance, from her spotless uniform to her flawless makeup and carefully arranged hair screamed perfection. If he hadn't been told she was the fragile looking woman in the bed hooked up to several machines and a nasal cannula, he wouldn't have believed it. Her entire head was wrapped in a sterile white bandage, and most of her visible skin was bruised or covered with cuts and abrasions.

"Elaine?" Maddie choked out, arriving at her partner's bedside. She touched the back of Elaine's hand with her fingertips.

Elaine opened her eyes, the irises startlingly blue in the bruised face.

"Maddie." The smokey voice sounded pained.

"Hey." Maddie swallowed. "I'm told we can't stay long. I was worried about you."

"I'm fine." Elaine stretched her lips in a smile. "But I saw him."

Trevor's eyes widened. He joined Maddie at the side of the bed. "You saw who?"

"The man who did...this. I think."

Her eyes closed.

They waited. She didn't open them again.

"Elaine?" Maddie said. No answer.

Trevor glanced at the machine showing her vitals. "I think she fell asleep."

A noise behind them had them both whirling to face the young nurse. She flushed. "Sorry. I didn't mean to startle you. It's time for you to go."

"She was talking and fell asleep," Maddie murmured.

"Yeah. We gave her a pretty strong sedative." She made a shooing gesture to hurry them out the door.

Maddie scowled. He knew that look. She had something she wanted to say but knew she shouldn't. Maddie wasn't known for her patience. Sooner or later, the words were going to be said. Trevor motioned toward the door. She left, her forceful stride indicating how irritated she was. She waited until they were out of earshot before the words shot out of her.

"Really? Come and tell us we have five minutes and she wants to see us, but don't tell us she's been given a sedative?" She glared in the direction of the ICU. "Had we known that we might have skipped the small talk and gotten her to tell us more about the man she saw."

"We have part of him on video."

She swung around to face him. "We do?"

He nodded. "The school has excellent security. Unfortunately, we can't see his face. If I had to guess, I'd say he knew exactly how far the cameras went and deliberately set himself on the edge, knowing we'd get enough to tease us."

Her eyes widened. "So, it's someone who is able to get into the school on a regular basis?"

"That's one possibility. Or maybe he's familiar with the security system they use. Whatever the answer is, there's more." He glanced uneasily around the lobby. There were a few people loitering about. But even one was too many.

"Look," he muttered, keeping his voice low. "I don't think this is the place to have this conversation. I have my truck parked right outside. What do you say to this: I can drive you to pick up your cruiser. We can talk on the way there."

She dipped her chin in a sharp nod. "Fine. But let's go quickly because I've had just about all I can take today. I need to get home to my daughters."

"Got it. Let's go."

They turned together towards the entrance. She hit a patch of water on the smooth surface and slipped. Instinctively, Trevor reached out to touch her elbow and steady her. She flinched back from him.

Her reaction shocked him. His jaw dropped.

Maddie flushed. "Sorry. I didn't mean to react like that. I don't like to be touched."

Trevor didn't say anything, but he was deeply troubled. Growing up, he and Maddie had always touched easily. Nothing flirtatious. A pat on the shoulder or a quick tap on the elbow just as a sign of support. Maybe if they were laughing about something, one of them might nudge the other with their shoulder or elbow. He had a feeling if he tried to nudge her with his shoulder right now, she would turn on him.

What had happened to the free-spirited girl he had grown up with? He wanted answers, but he knew that now was not the time. When they weren't in the middle of a hunt for this maniac, he would find out what happened to Maddie. Not because he was nosy, but because despite the distance she had placed between them when she had married, she was still important to him. If there was trouble in her life, he wanted her to know that he was there for her the way he'd always been.

Careful, his mind whispered. Maddie and Angie were the only girls Trevor had ever let in. And both of them had broken his heart. Angie when she died. And Maddie when she ghosted him and severed their friendship. He would never abandon Maddie in her time of need. But he needed to guard his heart. Something about her got under his skin, and he didn't want to risk that kind of heartache again.

Silently, they made their way out to his truck. The windows had been kept partly open. A gorgeous German Shepherd sat in the passenger seat wearing a K-9 work vest. Her tongue lolled out in a friendly canine grin when they approached.

Trevor pulled out his key fob and hit the unlock button twice. Although he wanted to open her door for her, he resisted. Instead, he opened the driver's side door and grabbed the lever so he could pull the backrest of his seat down, leaving room for Misty to get to the back.

He patted the seat in the back of the cab. "Here, Misty."

She obediently stood and hopped over the seat and positioned herself in the back. Maddie got into the passenger side, and Trevor slipped behind the wheel.

She snapped her seatbelt into place. "So, what was it you didn't want to say back there?"

He waited to answer until he was driving. "Here's what we know. The explosive was a homemade bomb. It was destroyed to the point it was difficult to see much. The school gave us access to all the footage from their security cameras. They are pretty state of the art, and we have multiple cameras with various views."

"That's good news."

He heard the question in her tone. If the cameras were so good, why wasn't he telling her the perp had been identified or caught?

"We saw the car in question pull in at 10:17 this morning. The vehicle has tinted windows, so we couldn't see the driver. Adding to that, he parked at the far end of the camera's reach. Literally, the front hood was all that we could see in the video."

"How is that even possible if the security was so great?"

Great question.

"They didn't go back far enough." She'd love the next part. "Later, we could see a person who was standing on the edge of the field vision. All we could see was his back and hands. He was wearing gloves, and he was nowhere near the car the bomb was in. When we looked at all of the videos together, we could see him take something from his pocket. It might have been a remote detonator."

She sucked in a breath. "The timing wasn't an accident. It was deliberate."

He glanced at her pale face. "It was. He waited until you and Elaine were within feet of the car before he pushed the button."

She cleared her throat. "So, was I the target or was Elaine?"

She held her breath and waited for Trevor to respond.

"I'm not sure. We don't even know if you were specifically targeted. He might have just waited until the kids were gone and an officer was within range."

She frowned. Her stomach was in knots. "Do you think it could have been that random?"

He shrugged, his hands tightening on the wheel. "I'm not sure of anything. All we know is you were the first officers to go past the car after the kids were gone. It could have just been your bad luck that you happened to be the ones."

"What is your gut telling you?" Trevor had always had great instincts.

He glanced her way again and pinned her briefly with his dark eyes. "Right now, my instinct is telling me to drive you as far as possible from this case. Which of course, I won't do. But Maddie, be careful. I've got a bad feeling about this."

So he believed she was the target.

"Was there anything about the man that might help us identify him."

"Not at the moment. We have no facial features, no identifiable scars or clothing. His long coat was so bulky, and there's no clear view of the perp's size. And since we can't see all of him, we don't even know his height. We are going to interview those who were on scene to see if anyone caught a better view."

"There were a lot of people standing around. Was he there when the kids and teachers were still at the school?"

"No. He moved into position after all the children and teachers were standing in the ballfield to wait for parents to pick up the kids."

"At least we know he didn't want to hurt them."

Her daughters hadn't been in danger. That time. But what if this man decided to have another go at someone else at the school. Or if she was the target, weren't her children the best way to get to her?

"They're not going back."

Her jaw ached. She'd been grinding her teeth. She opened her mouth and moved her jaw, trying to work out the pain.

"Who is not going back?"

She shifted in her seat so she could watch Trevor's profile. He had an expressive face. Every thought was reflected on it. Or it used to be when they were growing up. Now, he was more controlled.

"My twins. I refuse to send Piper and Paige back to the school until this guy is caught. Especially if there's really a chance he's after me. My kids would be targets."

"I don't blame you."

Something in her relaxed. She had expected him to argue, maybe question her judgment. Why did she continue to let Alex's flaws affect how she viewed others?

Sighing, she leaned her head back and closed her eyes. Weariness pressed down on her like a weighted blanket. The events of the day caught up with her. She shivered. Crossing her arms, she hugged them tight to her chest to keep warm.

The heater kicked on. Warm air rushed from the vents and hit her legs and face. Opening her eyes, she watched Trevor adjust the settings to high heat.

"Do you want the heated seat on?"

"Well, yeah."

He smiled and tapped the button twice, turning it on to the highest level.

"Thanks."

"You've always gotten cold after an emotional upset."

Even after all these years, he knew her so well. Part of her regretted allowing their friendship to lapse. Trevor had always had her back in the past. She especially recalled how helpful he'd been when her dad and older brother had been killed in a car accident when she was fifteen. Trevor had dropped everything to be with her. He ran errands for her mom, drove them to the funeral home, answered the phones and let her cry on his shoulder and talk for hours.

He didn't even pressure her when she refused to go back to church in the weeks after the accident, although she knew her decision bothered him.

Did he still go to church? Or had he grown bitter with life and stopped going, too?

It wasn't that she didn't believe in God. She did. But she had no room in her life for someone who didn't protect her when the worst happened.

Her phone buzzed. She shook herself out of her maudlin thoughts and opened the text. "My mom says they've settled down to watch a movie. All is well. Dinner will be at six." She hesitated over the next part. But she couldn't lie, even by omission. "Mom says you're invited, and she refuses to take no for an answer."

Trevor laughed. "Why would I say no to your mama's cooking? I'd have to go home and eat my own."

His quip surprised a snicker out of her. "You still can't cook?"

"I try," he protested. "Not everyone has the talent of the Blake women."

Talent. She grinned. "It's not that we're talented. You're just a bit of a disaster when it comes to cooking."

"Can't deny it. Can I bring Misty?"

In her peripheral vision, she saw the dog's ears perk up. "Someone knows she's being talked about."

"She's a smart pooch. What can I say?"

Maddie opened her mouth to make a snarky comment, then noticed their surroundings. All humor fled. The school was around the next corner. Sitting up, she firmed her jaw. What she wanted was to go check on her twins. But her mom had said they were fine.

Despite everything that had happened during the past few hours, Maddie refused to let fear have the upper hand. The Maddie Blake who'd been a victim of domestic abuse had survived and grown stronger. Now, she had a job to do. She wasn't off the clock until five. That left her two more hours to work on catching this creep who liked to build bombs and place them in school parking lots.

Chapter Four

The school looked like a graveyard when they arrived. Trevor cruised slowly past the high school located across the street from the elementary school. She checked his speedometer. He was driving exactly fifteen miles per hour. A group of young girls stood on the sidewalk in a circle, phones in hand, giggling and laughing. She frowned. Regardless of the fact that the bomb threat had been at the elementary school, the high school had been evacuated at the same time and all the students sent home. The two schools weren't on the same campus, but they were within sight of each other. The handbook she'd read at the beginning of the school year stated the entire district would go on lockdown in the event of any credible threat.

It amazed her to see students on the property so soon after an explosion.

Trevor pulled up to the curb next to the elementary school directly behind her cruiser. She shook her head. Was it really only four hours since she and Elaine got the emergency call? It felt like a week had passed. Her left side burned where she'd slammed against the ground, and pain gathered behind her eyes.

Squinting, she peered around. The rain had stopped, although a thick layer of dark clouds roamed through the gray sky. The late afternoon was eerily quiet. No cars. No students or teachers. None of the usual commotion one would expect to see on a Friday afternoon. Normally, there would be after school events or teachers who stayed late to finish up grading papers or write lesson plans. Or a cleaning crew.

Today, the parking lot was empty save for the emergency vehicles still working the scene.

Reluctantly, she twisted her head and saw the scorch marks left by the burning vehicle. Yellow crime scene tape surrounded the area. The vehicle itself had been removed. Investigators worked on photographing, tagging and carefully collecting what had been left of it after the explosion.

"I wonder how long it will take them to process the scene?" she mused. "If the majority of the car is gone, and the school has been gone through."

"Well," he started slowly, "Remember how I said the bomber stayed close enough to tease, but not close enough for us to identify?"

She nodded. "Yeah. So?"

"How'd he know?" He turned off the ignition and shifted so he faced her. "He knew exactly where the boundaries were. I find that suspicious. Don't you?"

Maddie felt like all the air had been sucked from inside the truck. "It's someone in the school."

"Possibly. Or someone who knows the security system a little too well."

She furrowed her brow, thinking. "Isn't it odd that the cameras have a blind spot? After all, isn't this supposed to be a state-of-the-art system?"

"Not necessarily. Covering the area outside is more challenging than one might think." He bumped the steering wheel lightly with his fist. "Regardless, the fact he stepped exactly on the edge of the camera's field of vision is too much of a coincidence. This was planned."

"I am definitely not sending my kiddos back until he's caught." She shuddered.

"I don't blame you. I'd do the same thing."

She put her hand on the door to open it, then paused. "Trevor?"

"Huh?"

"If he's after me, what would stop him from putting a bomb on my cruiser after everyone left the scene?"

His gaze slowly turned toward her, his expression darkening. Then he narrowed his eyes and scanned her car and the surrounding area. Finally, he relaxed. "I think you're safe. After all, look how many people are still combing the scene? Not to mention, if he knows the system like I think he does, then he'd know your cruiser is in the camera's range. I could clearly see it when I watched the videos this afternoon."

She blew out her breath, hard. Well, that was a relief. "Yeah. I think I'm just a bit jumpy."

It wasn't only the bomb, though. She'd been a victim before. And even though she'd rescued herself and her children, the nightmare she'd lived through would never leave her. Every once in a while, she got panicky.

"Just to be on the safe side," he opened his door and stepped out of the truck. "Misty, come."

The German Shepherd climbed over the seat and lightly jumped down from the cab. Then she waited at attention for his orders.

He led the K-9 over to the cruiser. "Misty, seek."

Maddie clenched her fists and sat in the cab of the truck watching the dog at work. She wasn't used to being an observer. She preferred to take an active role. However, in this case, she'd be in the way. Not to mention, she felt a little emotionally compromised.

Misty completed her search and returned to Trevor's side. Maddie's shoulders sagged. Apparently, the K-9 hadn't found anything suspicious. Relief filtered through her. She could take her vehicle, pick up her children and go home.

With a renewed sense of energy, she shoved her door open and slipped out of the front seat, taking care not to place her foot in the deep puddle Trevor had parked next to. She still managed to find a patch of mud. Her foot hit it and sank down.

"Ugh! Now I'll have to clean my boots tonight." She jerked her foot out of the mud. It made a disgusting sucking sound. Yuck. She strode over to her cruiser. "Well, I'm glad this isn't rigged."

He smiled and stepped away from the vehicle. "Are you heading home?"

She shrugged. It felt odd exchanging small talk as if they hadn't had years of almost zero contact. Still, she had been raised to be polite. "Nah, I plan on heading into the station first and dropping this off..."

Her voice petered out as she realized her current situation.

"What?"

She shook her head frowning. "It's nothing." She sighed, frustrated. "Only, my car needed some work, so it's in the shop. Elaine had picked me up and driven me to work. I don't have a vehicle stashed there."

"No big deal. I'll follow you to the station. I need to talk with the lieutenant for a moment anyhow. Then I'll give you a ride home. Or to your mom's. Wherever."

"Really?" She raised her eyebrows at him. "I don't want to inconvenience you, but it would help me out a lot."

"No problem. Like I said, I want to talk with Lieutenant Marshall anyway."

She nodded. They so rarely saw each other that she'd forgotten the bomb squad was quartered on the same campus as the other police officers. Though they all did a monthly training together.

"If you're sure, I'd really appreciate it."

"Misty, in the truck."

The dog trotted back to the truck and stood at the driver's side door, her tongue hanging out in a canine grin. She was a gorgeous dog.

"You go ahead. I'll load Misty up, and we'll follow you back to the station."

She didn't need to be told twice. Glancing back at the school that had seemed such a safe place this morning, she shivered. It would forever be shadowed by menace, at least in her mind.

Unlocking the vehicle, she slid behind the wheel. The entire drive to the station, she tried to keep her mind off the empty passenger seat. Her aggravation with her partner seemed so minor and unimportant now. What did it matter if Elaine stuffed a napkin or two in the door? It wasn't like they didn't clean out all the garbage at the end of every shift. Elaine was a solid cop with a sterling reputation. She didn't deserve to be caught in an explosion or the recipient of someone's malicious murder attempt.

From now on, Maddie promised herself she'd make an effort to be more patient and less exacting in her dealings with her partner.

Poor Elaine. An image of the usually put together blonde in the narrow hospital bed surrounded by machines intruded into Maddie's thoughts. She winced. She was alive. And the hospital staff had seemed to feel she'd recover. Still, Maddie shifted restlessly in her seat. She wished there was more she could do for her.

Mom would suggest she pray for Elaine. *Yeah, not ready to do that.* Maddie had learned too well that prayer didn't help. After all, her husband had still been controlling and abusive. God hadn't stopped that situation. Maddie herself had done that. Nor had God kept her dad and brother alive.

No. They could only depend on themselves. Setting her jaw, she pulled into the LaMar Pond Police Department. She would get a ride home with Trevor and call her mom to bring her kids to them.

And what of Trevor? Despite the way they'd met up, it had been easy, too easy, to pick up the rhythm of how they used to chat before Alex had wormed his way into her life. She enjoyed his company, always had. But allowing Trevor back into her life might complicate things. Not because of their former friendship.

Today, she had seen him as more than an old pal. He'd been competent, strong and comfortable in his role as a protector. A man a woman could become attracted to and fall for. Not that she was at risk. Even if she hadn't realized before today how handsome and rugged he'd become, she was not in the market for any kind of relationship.

But just to be on the safe side, she couldn't risk renewing their friendship. Her priority had to be raising her daughters.

That, and catching the man who'd tried to murder her and her partner.

*

Trevor pulled in beside Maddie then took a moment to gather his thoughts together. He needed to update his commander on Elaine and the possibility that she may be able to identify the suspect. In addition, he wanted to check and see if the team had made any progress on the case since he'd left to check on Maddie and Elaine.

He got out of the vehicle and stood back so Misty could jump down. She hit the ground and stood at his side, tail wagging while he picked up his cell phone and slid it into his pocket. Then he locked the door. Pushing his glasses up his nose, he and Misty moved toward Maddie.

The moment she glanced his way, Trevor sensed the wall she'd placed between them. He ground his teeth. Why was she so set on holding him at a distance? Trevor had been her best friend for years. He'd seen her in all her moods. No one knew her like he did.

Maybe that was the problem.

Whatever the issue was, he didn't have time to deal with it. He needed to find this guy. He wasn't sure if Maddie and Elaine had been the absolute target or if the man had been sending a general message.

Did they even know if it was a man? He thought so. Most bombers were, although not all. Plus, Elaine had thought she'd seen a man. They needed to move fast on that information. The moment she was out of her drug-induced sleep, someone needed to be there getting her statement and a profile started.

That someone would not be him. He needed to get his hands on the remains of the explosive and go over them again. He had a feeling they'd missed something, but there were so many holes in this case, that went without saying.

"How long before you're ready to head home?"

She ran a hand through her red hair, brushing it behind her ear. "Not long. I guess the question is how long do you need to confer with your lieutenant?"

Trevor lifted his phone and checked the time. "I know he'll be officially off the clock in twenty minutes."

"Yeah, but how often does he actually pay attention to that?" She scoffed.

"You're not wrong. He often stays late, but I don't want to keep him waiting. You should probably let Chief Kennedy know about Elaine's condition and what she saw."

"You're right. Call me when you're ready to go." She rattled off her cell phone number and he plugged it into his phone, then sent her a test text. When she got it, she added him to her contacts.

He called for Misty to come. When the faithful K-9 stood and waited for his next command, he gave the order to follow and separated from Maddie. She didn't even wave as she headed up the steps to the main entrance of the police station. He couldn't help but look over his shoulder once to watch her march towards her destination.

No matter how much time had passed since he last spoke with her, his pulse still spiked when she entered his vision. Such reactions were unproductive. And unwise. He'd missed their friendship. But the feelings she stirred weren't the same he had for his friends. He had to be careful. His track record with women stunk. He couldn't let himself fall for her. Shaking thoughts of her out of his mind, he sped up and typed the passcode into the security panel.

Before going to see the lieutenant, he dropped Misty off to be looked over and fed. The precinct had been awarded a grant to start up a K-9 training program. Although most of the animals were still puppies too young to be active officers, hopefully they'd have a small team in the near future. In the meantime, he'd been given the go ahead to have Misty cared for after working a scene. She'd get a clean bill of health, a grooming and a meal. He didn't think this was normal protocol at other departments, but Misty was the only full-time K-9, and they were proud of her. It would be interesting to see what the program looked like once they had more dogs certified.

Moving through the main room, he crossed between desks, responding to the greetings and jokes yelled out to him. A grin spread across his face. Trevor had always been a little on the shy side, but once he became a member of the LaMar Pond Bomb Squad, he'd found a family. It took a full five minutes to get through the room and reach the office he wanted.

He rapped once on the lieutenant's door. Immediately, Lieutenant Marshall bade him to enter.

There wasn't a lot of new information. The bomb had been mostly destroyed. They did know it was set off by remote detonator.

"Sir, Sergeant Cardon was awake briefly. Before she fell asleep again, she said she saw the bomber at the scene."

Lieutenant Marshall straightened in his chair. His intense gaze bore into Trevor. "Did she give anything we can use?"

"Not yet. But once she comes around again, hopefully she'll tell us something."

The lieutenant reached for the phone and began dialing. "Kennedy needs to be made aware of this stat."

Trevor continued to stand before the desk, his hands loosely folded behind his back, while Lieutenant Marshall talked with Chief Kennedy. He could only hear one side of the conversation, but he gathered enough to speculate that Chief Kennedy had already been informed that Elaine might have seen the person who set the bomb off. No doubt Maddie had told him as soon as she got into the station. After two minutes or so, the call ended. Marshall sat deep in thought. Trevor waited patiently, making no move to hurry his boss along. Eventually, he would tell Trevor what the next move was. Until then, Trevor had no choice but to wait.

He hoped Maddie wasn't expecting him to be done anytime soon, because judging from the expression on Marshall's face, he might be a while.

Lieutenant Marshall stood abruptly, startling Trevor from his thoughts.

"Sergeant Stone," he said. "Do we have any idea yet who or what the bomber's target was?"

Trevor shook his head. "No, sir. However, I do think it's important to remember that he did not set off the explosive until Sergeant Blake and Sergeant Cardon walked past."

"I agree." Lieutenant Marshall began to pace behind his desk. He often did this while he planned. "I would like to know specifically if he was targeting one of those women. Let's gather everyone who's on site and put it together. Meet in the conference room in ten."

And just like that, his plans of leaving quickly vanished. Trevor grabbed a Mountain Dew before heading to the conference room. On the way there, he sent Maddie a text.

Might be a minute. Team meeting. Hopefully she wouldn't be upset. His phone buzzed.

LOL. The Chief and Lt have been talking. We're going into a meeting, too. Text when you are sprung.

Grinning, he pocketed his phone and made his way to the conference room. There were five other team members present. Trevor set his Mountain Dew on the table and then pulled a chair out and swung it backwards before sitting on it, resting his forearms on the back. Sergeant Olivia Sanchez and Officer Gary Hollister sat on either side of him.

"Bruh," Gary pointed at his can. "You bring me one? You still owe me one."

Trevor pulled a can from his coat pocket and handed it to his buddy. "I looked at the chart you keep. It was my turn."

"You got that right."

"You guys are weird." Olivia rolled her eyes. "Just bring your own."

All the chatter froze the second Lieutenant Marshall entered the room and stood at the head of the table. "Okay, team, let's see what we've got. Stone, bring everyone up to speed."

Trevor went through everything he and the lieutenant had discussed. Gary raised his hand as if he was in elementary school.

"How would he know they'd be there, sir?" he asked. "What guarantee did he have that those particular officers would respond?"

"True. So the theory we're going with is that he planned to take out law enforcement personnel in general."

Trevor nodded. "That makes sense. When we looked at the video, after the children were gone, Maddie, I mean Sergeants Blake and Cardon, were the first officers to pass that way."

He flushed. But why? It's not like the lieutenant didn't know the two officers. They all knew each other. The fact that he said Maddie's name in front of his lieutenant didn't mean anything personal. It only felt that way. He cleared his throat. "The other question I have is why would he do this at a school?"

Lieutenant Marshall stopped and faced him. "This all feels like a very elaborate plan. He plants the bomb, keeping out of range, so, like we talked about earlier, he knows the system and where its weak points are."

Trevor picked up the narrative. "And then he waits until the kids and teachers are off campus and only the police, firefighters and emergency responders are close to the explosives."

Olivia rapped her fingers on the table. "I had wondered when the bomb first went off if it exploded late. But after we found it and saw that it was operated by remote detonator and then watching the video, that no longer makes sense. He obviously planned to do it when cops would be the ones hurt."

"Exactly." Trevor wiped the condensation from his can on a napkin. "Was he specifically after cops? I mean, would he have tried to take out firefighters or paramedics?" Around him, his colleagues continued to debate. His stomach bottomed out as another thought hit him.

"What if the bomber did know that Sergeant Blake and her partner would respond?" he blurted. All conversation broke off, and everyone stared at him.

"Explain." Lieutenant Marshall placed his palms on the table and leaned in. "How would he know?"

Trevor swallowed. "Sergeant Blake's twin daughters, Paige and Piper, are first graders at LaMar Pond Elementary School. Even if they were not on duty, there's no way she and Elaine wouldn't have responded to that call."

Chapter Five

Olivia made a scoffing sound. "That's a pretty big coincidence, Trevor. He plants a bomb, and she and Elaine just happen to be the first ones to cross his path? Too neat."

Trevor shrugged. "Maybe."

He couldn't shake the feeling, though. His instincts screamed at him that Maddie was in danger, no matter how unlikely it seemed.

"Wait a minute." The lieutenant held up his hands. "We can't dismiss the possibility that they were targets. Nor can we ignore other possibilities. Police officers have enemies. Anyone in law enforcement racks up a list of people who want them dead."

"But how many of those people would actually act on that hatred?" Olivia bit her lip.

Gary tossed his empty can like a basketball. It clattered into the recycling bin. "One is all it takes."

"Let's stay focused, people." Lieutenant Marshall scanned their faces, meeting each pair of eyes with his own. "Chief Kennedy wants us to meet with his team as soon as he finishes with his commander. I want us to have something productive to share when we come together with his people."

"Sir!" A young woman who worked at the reception desk ran into the room. "Sir, Channel 15...you've got to see this!"

Lieutenant Marshall grabbed the remote control for the large flatscreen television mounted on the wall and turned it on quickly, punching in the numbers for the news channel. Trevor's jaw dropped. The cute little nurse who had guided them to Elaine's room in the Intensive Care Unit was being interviewed.

"That's the nurse we saw at the hospital!" he exclaimed. "She was with us when Elaine..."

He stopped talking. That little nurse was breaking every rule of confidentiality he could think of.

"Oh, yes! Sergeant Elaine Cardon is in our ICU. A bomb went off at the elementary school, and she nearly died. She's in serious condition. Her partner came in to see her today, and Sergeant Cardon told her she'd seen the man who did it!"

"Did you hear the description of the bomber?" The reporter leaned in, avid eyes and greedy smile focused on the girl.

"Well, not everything." She twirled a hand of hair around her fingers. "I didn't hear the whole conversation. I was in and out of the room. But I'm sure she told her partner. I'll bet they catch this guy tonight!"

Then the entire team listened, horrified, as the young girl continued to give information that no one except the police or Elaine's family should have.

"Someone's going to be out of a job super quick," Olivia muttered darkly. "And did she just hint that she heard part of the bomber's description? Didn't you say that Elaine fell asleep before she could give you or her partner a description?"

Trevor didn't trust himself to speak. He nodded at Olivia. This was so much worse than someone risking their employment.

"That kid just put a target on her own back," Gary bit out.

The lieutenant switched off the television, his expression grim. The sound of breathing was the only thing disturbing the deep silence that fell on the room. They all recognized the harm that one seemingly innocent interview had done.

The conference room phone rang. The lieutenant glanced at the caller ID and answered, putting it on speaker.

"Hey Paul. Marshall here. I'm with the team. You're on speaker."

"Good, that saves time." Paul Kennedy's gravelly voice filled the room. "I'm hoping you saw the news?"

"Yeah. We caught most of it." The lieutenant responded.

"That woman put some of our people at risk." The chief stated. "And probably herself, as well."

"I agree. If this guy sees the interview, he'll think both Elaine and Maddie can identify him."

"Best case scenario, which is not a good one by the way, he'll think we're on to him and run. Which means we might have just lost our chance to catch him."

Lieutenant Marshall rubbed his eyes with the heel of his hand. "Or he could decide Elaine and Maddie are risks he can't afford."

"I'm putting officers on Elaine at the hospital. They're heading out that way within minutes."

"What about the nurse?"

"We'll have to put someone on her, too."

If she still has a job. Trevor kept the thought to himself.

"And Maddie?"

Trevor sat up. Maddie needed protection, too.

"With Elaine out of service, I am a little short—"

"Sir!" Trevor burst out, shocking himself.

Apparently, he shocked everyone else, too. They all stared at him. Trevor was not one to interrupt a conversation.

"Yes, Sergeant Stone?" The lieutenant's voice was mild. Trevor couldn't tell if he was annoyed or not. At the moment, though, he didn't care. His heart pounded in his chest. The blood pumped through his veins so hard he could barely hear anything else.

Maddie, his Maddie, was in trouble. Possibly a new target for someone who'd already nearly taken her out. There was no way he could sit silently when she needed protection. And what about her kids? If anything happened to Paige, Piper or Amanda, it would devastate her. He didn't know if she'd ever recover.

Nor would he be able to live with himself if he sat here listening and did nothing. This was more than a matter of honor. To not speak up went against everything he believed to be right and proper as a man, as an officer and as a child of God.

"Sorry for interrupting, Chief. Lieutenant. But Maddie has twins that go to that school. If she was a target, he'd know about them and Maddie. And if she wasn't, he'll be highly motivated to learn about her now."

"Yes, you have a point," the chief said, his voice suddenly weary.

"I've known Maddie all my life. She and I are both going to be working on this case. Why don't we partner up while Elaine's out of commission? Maybe send her daughters and mother somewhere they'll be safe. That way she won't worry about them, and we can focus on putting this guy behind bars."

Silence fell while both commanding officers contemplated the plan. The chief came to a decision first.

"I think that sounds like a great plan," Chief Kennedy boomed.

The lieutenant agreed, but not before giving Trevor a steady gaze. Trevor kept himself from squirming under the level stare, but it was a close call. He felt like a teenager caught sneaking out.

When the lieutenant hung up the phone, the group spent a few more minutes strategizing. "Sergeant Stone, get Misty, and then I need you and Maddie to figure out where her family can go to keep them safe until this individual is caught."

*

Maddie was sitting at her desk when he entered the police station thirty minutes later. When she glanced up at him, he could see that she'd been shaken by the news. She didn't look angry. It went deeper than that. When those hazel eyes met his, he was happy to see none of the rage seemed to be directed at him.

"Are you okay?" Inwardly, he winced. What a stupid question. Of course, she wasn't.

"Not even close." She pushed back her chair and stood. "I listened to that interview, and I couldn't decide if that little nurse was naïve, selfish or just plain clueless."

"Maybe a little of all three. Although I'm sure she's already learned a tough lesson. Or will soon. The hospital is pretty strict about confidentiality."

She snorted. "If she's not fired without a reference, I'll be astonished. But that doesn't solve the bigger issue. Lily Shepherd, one of our officers, and her partner Mac headed to the hospital to keep watch over Elaine. The chief notified the nurse and her family that she might be in trouble. She refused any protection. Can you believe it? Literally laughed at the chief on the phone and told him he was trying to intimidate her."

"Unbelievable."

She nodded. "Right? But we can't do anything if she refuses protection."

"What about your family? Are they safe?"

"They are. I called my mom. She and the girls are headed to my Uncle Joe's tonight. Joe is a cop in Michigan. So are his sons, my cousins Zane and Zeke. They'll protect Mom and the girls."

He raised an eyebrow. "Zane and Zeke?"

For a brief second, a smile flittered across her face, quickly chased away by shadows. "Yeah. Twins. They run in my family."

"Will he call you when they arrive?"

"Someone will. But it won't be for a while. It's a 6-hour drive."

"Then there's nothing more we can do about them." He shoved his hands in his coat pockets. "Should we head back to your place?"

She quirked an eyebrow, clearly asking a question.

"Maddie, I don't intend on leaving you on your own. And both our bosses agree. We can act as partners on the case, and we'll stick together."

*

Maddie frowned. She didn't need a babysitter. As long as her mom and her twins were out of danger, she was fine. She opened her mouth to tell him so. When he held up his hands as if warding off an attack, she sniffed to hold a laugh in. She'd seen that gesture so many times. Trevor Stone thought of himself as a shy, non-confrontational man. He thought he was placating her. Well, she'd learned long ago that shy, self-effacing Trevor had a backbone of iron and didn't let go of an idea once it got stuck in his head as the right thing to do.

"Hear me out."

She rolled her eyes but gestured for him to continue. After all, he was going to say what was on his mind anyway.

"You know as well as I do that the interview put a target on your back. Now I don't care how we do it. But we are sticking together."

He folded his arms across his chest, waiting for her to argue, she was sure of it.

Weariness settled over Maddie like a concrete blanket. She could hardly hold her head up under the weight. For once, it would be nice having someone around who was one hundred percent on her side. An equal who wouldn't complain about simple things.

Someone she knew would have her back. It had been so long since she'd allowed herself to trust and share her burdens and fears. It was a short-term solution. She couldn't let herself rely on him forever. But what would a few days hurt?

Plus, Chief Kennedy had stressed how stretched the department was. Trevor's watching her would mean they could focus on guarding Elaine and catching this bomber before he succeeded in killing someone.

She sighed. "Okay."

He blinked, looking like a startled owl with big eyes behind his dark framed glasses.

She held back a snicker. She'd missed his expressions.

"Really? You agree, just like that? I was sure I'd have to get down on my knees and beg."

"Maybe I was too hasty."

"Nope. Can't take it back now." The humor fled from his face. "Seriously. I have Misty waiting in the truck. What do you want to do?"

She rubbed the back of her neck. "I don't want to stay at my place. Not without the twins. Being there will do nothing but make me think of them and my mom all night. I am exhausted."

"That's fine. We can go to my place. I have a security system. You can stay in the guest room. I promise you'll have plenty of privacy. Or we can go somewhere else."

She frowned and thought. "No. I think your house will be fine. But I'd like to do something first."

"Anything."

His quick reply eased some of the strain twisting her gut. She was so tired of fighting for everything. "I know it's silly. Mac and Lily are with her. But I want to stop in and see Elaine again."

"We can do that."

She gathered up her purse and her coat and followed him outside. Neither spoke again until they were in his truck. Misty woofed a quiet greeting. She ruffled the dog's ears. When this was over, maybe she'd get a dog. The girls would love that. Alex had been allergic to dogs, so they hadn't gotten one when they'd married. Once she'd left him, she was too busy looking over her shoulder. Then as a single mother working full-time, she didn't have the time to care for a pet properly.

But once things settled down again, she'd investigate buying a dog. Getting a dog, or a pet of any kind, required a certain level of commitment. It also declared she was ready to move forward with her life.

It was about time.

"Thanks for agreeing to this," she said. "I know we were there earlier today. And I'm sure the hospital will call if there's a change. But I appreciate it."

Trevor glanced at her, his gaze slightly narrowed. She knew that look. He was trying to get a better read on her thoughts.

"I don't mind. I didn't think you two were friends."

She heard the question in his voice. "We're not." Stretching out her legs, she allowed the heat from the vent to warm them. "Elaine's only been with us for about six months. She's a good cop. Efficient and smart. But she has a bit of a superior attitude. It hasn't endeared her to anyone. Truthfully, she's my partner, and I can't think of anyone who is her friend."

"No one? That's sad."

A sliver of guilt sliced into her. She should have been the first to befriend Elaine. After all, they were partners. Sighing, she responded to his statement.

"True. I haven't been there for her like I should have been, and it shames me. She lives alone. And as far as I know, she has no close family. I know it's not necessary, and she has a guard, but I want her to know she's not alone."

Trevor reached over and placed his hand on top of hers. Then he removed it so rapidly she half wondered if she'd imagined it. But the skin on the back of her hand tingled like she'd been zapped with electricity. It was no dream. He hadn't meant it as anything more than a friendly gesture. So why was her pulse jumping around? And her face was on fire.

Desperate to hide the blush covering her cheeks, she turned her head as if she wanted to peer out the window. There was nothing to see. It was still rainy and overcast.

She clenched her hands together on her lap so he couldn't put his hand over hers again. She caught his glance. He knew what she was doing and why. She was sure of it. But she ignored the ridiculous urge to put her arm back on the center arm rest. She couldn't afford to forget that Trevor was a colleague and nothing more. It didn't matter how his nearness affected her or the way his voice soothed her like melted honey eased an aching throat.

She didn't want to give her heart any more reasons to act up. Trevor wasn't a boyfriend. She wasn't even sure she could still call him a friend, not after she'd kicked him to the curb so many years ago.

But he was here. And he was acting the part of her best friend, as if he'd never been hurt by her rejection.

She knew he had been. Every once in a while, they'd see each other, and he had never been able to completely hide the hurt when she'd look right through him as if they'd never been more than colleagues. Even now, she sensed a hesitation and guardedness he'd never shown around her before. Like how he'd snatched his hand away so quickly rather than letting it stay as a show of comfort and support. That bothered her. But she wasn't ready to examine why. By all rights, he could have done his duty and walked away. She knew he'd volunteered to work with her as a partner to close this case.

It humbled her, given how poorly she'd treated him.

He'd stepped up to help as if none of that mattered.

It did, though. She couldn't let herself forget it. No matter who he was, she couldn't allow a man into her life again. One had nearly destroyed her.

And then there was his faith.

She knew Trevor Stone was a man who lived by his faith.

He was also the person who'd been there when she'd rejected hers.

She and Trevor were two people who shouldn't be more than colleagues. As soon as this case ended, their association would end. Again. Just thinking about pushing him out of her life hurt. She knew now that she'd always miss him. His absence would leave a Trevor shaped hole inside her soul.

But it would be for the best. She'd get a dog and raise her daughters alone and try to forget the part of her heart that was beginning to yearn for Trevor Stone.

Chapter Six

They were less than two miles from the hospital when her cell phone rang. She pulled it out and glanced at the name. She swallowed down a stab of apprehension. Just because he called her so soon after she left the station didn't mean anything had gone wrong.

Of course, it also didn't mean he had anything good to share.

"It's the chief." She forced her voice to remain level and matter of fact. Then she swiped her finger on the touchscreen to accept the call. "Hi, Chief."

"Maddie. I have some bad news." Her gut clenched at the serious tone. "Is Sergeant Stone with you?"

"Yes, sir. Trevor's right beside me. We're driving." She stopped talking when the last word wobbled.

Trevor cast a quick glance in her direction.

"Good. Please put your phone on speaker."

Immediately, she held the phone away from her ear and did so. "Done. We can both hear you."

"Thank you. I just got off the phone with a very distraught mother. The young nurse who caused so much trouble is dead. She was found shot to death in her car less than an hour ago."

Maddie's breath caught in her throat. She hadn't expected that, but she wasn't shocked. The young woman had made herself a target and then refused protection. If only she'd allowed them to guard her. She might have acted unwisely, but she hadn't deserved to die.

Maddie shoved the emotional response aside. She had a job to do in order to bring the young nurse's killer to justice. "Give me the address. Trevor and I will head out that direction."

Each word dropped from her mouth, hard and brittle.

"Plug the address into my phone," Trevor whispered. She nodded and did as he asked. The truck's GPS system recalibrated.

"Chief, I have the address in the GPS. We'll arrive approximately fifteen minutes from now."

"Good. Maddie, I already have people processing the scene. I want you to take point on talking to the parents. Their names are Fred and Honey Olden. They have another daughter, Gretchen. The deceased daughter was Mercy, aged twenty-two."

"Will do." She didn't ask why. She already knew. People tended to open up to her more than they did to her colleagues. If the nurse had said anything to her parents that might lead to her killer, they'd be more likely to tell her than another officer.

"Are you okay doing this?"

She peered at Trevor. "What do you mean?"

He flipped the blinker on and waited for a car to pass before turning left. His eyes met hers for a moment. Outside, the sky was growing dim, the horizon glowing orange and pink. The heavy clouds continued to block the sky, minimizing any light from the moon or stars. It was close to six-thirty in the evening. Her stomach rumbled, reminding her she hadn't eaten since she'd stopped for lunch with Elaine. She couldn't do anything about that now. A family needed her.

"I mean are you okay to go and talk with this family?"

She'd forgotten his question. "Yeah. I guess. Why wouldn't I be?"

She knew Trevor well enough to know he wasn't questioning her ability as a police officer. In fact, of all the people in her life, Trevor had always seemed to believe in her the most, telling her that despite her trouble staying still, she could still do anything she wanted if she set her mind to it.

She recalled confessing to him once that she thought she might have ADHD. Fidgeting was a symptom. In fact, even now, as she sat in his truck cab, her left leg continued to bounce. In class, unless especially interested in the subject matter, Maddie got distracted and needed to fidget with something to keep her mind on the lessons. And she was often restless and sometimes she acted impulsively. Although she'd gotten better over the years. She'd finally been diagnosed in high school, but her mother had refused to put her on medication.

Maddie watched her children carefully for signs of ADHD. So far, there'd been no concerns.

Trevor had listened and agreed it was a possibility but had continued to support her. In fact, he was the one who'd said keeping something to fidget with in class might help. She'd been touched to learn he'd done some research on his own when she'd admitted her worries.

That was the kind of friend Trevor Stone had always been.

She'd missed him.

She refocused on their conversation.

"You've been through a lot today. There was a bomb scare at your kids' school, you were nearly killed, your partner is in the hospital, your family is at risk, and now you're going to interview the parents of a young murder victim."

She felt her anxiety rising with each word. She blinked her eyes. She would not cry. "Stop. I get it. And you are right. But I can't think about it now. I don't want to go and talk to the parents. I want to call my mom and Paige and Piper. Then I want to check on Elaine before I crawl into bed and cry myself to sleep."

She bit her lip hard enough to taste blood. Had she really just admitted that? So much for maintaining her professional demeanor. Only Trevor could make her confess those feelings. Squirming, she tried to think of something to say to ease the awkward silence.

"It's okay. You know you can trust me." There was no judgment in his tone. Only the steady warmth she'd come to expect from him.

Something settled in her soul. She did. Suddenly, an odd urge struck her. So odd, she tried to shove it away. But it wouldn't budge. She hadn't felt such an urge for years. But it was there. She fought against it for thirty seconds before giving in.

"Trevor?"

"Yeah?"

She swallowed and gathered her courage. "Would you...do you think you could say a prayer for me? For this situation?"

By the time the words left her mouth, her entire face burned. She wished she could pull the question back.

Trevor sat silently for a long five seconds. "Of course I can. It would be my honor."

It didn't escape her notice how rough his voice was, as if he was struggling with some strong emotion.

He reached out to her. Without thinking, she placed her hand in his and felt the warmth of his skin sink into hers. For a second, she panicked. She was in an enclosed place with a man, and he had her hand. He could—

Wait. It was Trevor. Trevor who had held her when she screamed out her grief for her dead father and brother.

Trevor who had stood between her and the school bully who went after Maddie because she was jealous of her hair color.

And then he began to pray. Maddie hadn't listened to anyone pray in over a decade. They were only words, but she felt them drop on her bruised heart like kisses from Heaven. A gentle peace, one she hadn't felt for years, filled her.

It suddenly struck her. She'd abandoned God. Was it possible that He hadn't abandoned her, but had been waiting for her to welcome Him back? She bowed her head and let the prayer wash over her while tears leaked from her eyes.

*

Trevor would never recall the prayer he uttered. He was aware of Maddie crying beside him, but then she became still. Worry tightened in his chest. Was she well? Maybe he shouldn't have pushed her. But Maddie had always been so strong.

"Turn left. Your destination will be on the right."

Beside him, Maddie raised her head and wiped her sleeve across her face.

"Maddie—"

She turned to face him and smiled. His voice stuttered to a halt. He couldn't recall ever seeing his Maddie smile that way.

"Thanks Trevor. I needed that."

Needed what? The prayer? Time to cry and let some of the emotional pressure out? She did seem different. Before she'd been so tense, he'd expected her to blow at any moment. She'd always been a bit volatile.

He pulled up in front of the house. All the lights were on.

"Is this her house?" He frowned. "I don't see any police or crime scene tape."

She sat forward. The dashboard lights highlighted the deep furrows on her forehead. "I don't either." She glanced at the address. "Maybe the chief sent the wrong address."

"Or maybe he sent us to the home while others process the scene."
Trevor pointed at a car in the driveway. The streetlights were bright
enough to make out the "Proud Parent of a Nurse" bumper sticker
on the rear window. "I'd say we have the correct house."

"Let's go." She pushed open the door. "I so don't want to do this."

She'd muttered the words so low, he wasn't sure he was meant to
hear them. But before he could say anything, she got out and shut
the door gently. That was Maddie. Her duty to others overrode her
personal preferences.

He commanded Misty to wait, then followed Maddie to the front
door. A man who appeared to be in his early fifties met them. His
shoulders were stooped with grief, and his face still showed the ravages
left by many tears.

"Sergeant Blake?" His voice was like sandpaper. Was it his normal
voice, or was it the effect of tears?

"Yes, sir. I'm sorry for your loss. This is my...partner, Sergeant
Stone. May we talk with you?"

He nodded and stepped back to allow them to pass. Upon entering,
Trevor heard weeping and quiet voices coming from further back in
the house.

"Chief Kennedy said you'd be stopping by," the distraught father
said. "My wife and older daughter are waiting in the kitchen."

Maddie took a deep breath and straightened her shoulders. She
seemed to be bracing herself for the horrendous duty they'd been sent
to complete. Correction. *She'd* been sent to complete. When the man
indicated with his hand a room off to the left, she proceeded them
down the hallway and entered the room.

In all his years in the police force, Trevor's job had never put him
in the position of interviewing the family of someone who had been
killed. The thought of doing so now curdled his stomach. He hadn't

lost very many people in his life. His parents were both still alive in Florida, where they had retired a few years before. He had no brothers or sisters. The only people he'd ever lost to death had been his grandparents, and he had been so young when they'd died that he barely recalled them.

This was not an experience he looked forward to. However, Trevor never shirked his duty. Nor would he ever abandon Maddie when she needed him.

Even if she'd done so to him. He still didn't know why. The thought reminded him of the need to step carefully. Maddie had clearly held him at a distance earlier. She hadn't shown signs of wanting to revisit their friendship. The only reason he was with her now was to help her and her family. He couldn't get used to having her around.

But it would be so easy to let her in again.

He couldn't afford it. Maddie Blake was the one woman he could fall for if he let his guard down.

Maddie sat next to the mother at the table. Her husband sat on the other side, and the daughter hovered at her mother's shoulder. Trevor lowered himself into the chair next to Maddie's trying to be as unobtrusive as possible.

"Mr. and Mrs. Olden, we are sorry for your loss. My partner and I met your daughter earlier today. She was a lovely girl. Very outgoing and friendly."

Trevor nodded in agreement. Maddie gave the impression that she had truly liked the girl. No hint of her frustration with Mercy seeped into her voice.

Honey sobbed once before biting on her clenched fist. Her shoulders continued to shake.

"This was because of that interview she did, wasn't it?" Gretchen snarled. "Is it because the police didn't do their jobs?"

"Gretchen!" Fred intervened. "That's not fair."

"It's not fair that my sister is dead!"

Maddie's eyes blazed with compassion. "You're right. It's not fair."

Gretchen jerked her head around and stared at Maddie. Probably shocked that she'd agree.

"What happened?" Fred asked, throwing his daughter a pleading glance.

"Sir, someone planted a bomb at a school and detonated it during school hours." She didn't mention she'd been injured when the bomb went off, Trevor noted.

Gretchen's eyes dropped to the floor.

Honey locked her eyes on Maddie. Tears continued to drip down her cheeks.

"Whoever did that, that's who attacked your daughter. We are investigating and following every lead. Putting this criminal in jail is our highest priority. If your daughter said or did anything that might be linked to this, it might help us."

They remained an hour in the house. Trevor marveled at how instinctively Maddie knew what to say. The family admitted that their daughter had called and told them she'd be on the news. She'd called the station and told them she had information about something that had happened. They hadn't known about the bombing until they saw her interview. But after the news aired, Mercy had called back, sobbing, saying the hospital had fired her.

"I was so worried when she called," Gretchen whispered. "I told her she shouldn't have said she might know something about the bomber. Why didn't the police do anything to protect her?"

"She told them not to," Honey responded, surprising Trevor. He thought, given Gretchen's accusations, that Mercy hadn't told her parents about that.

"Mom! You never told me that."

"I never got the chance. And then it was too late."

"She texted less than thirty minutes after she was fired," Gretchen murmured, obviously shaken by her mother's revelation. "Said she wouldn't go back to the hospital if they begged her. Someone had approached her and told her they were writing a book about bombings. They wanted her input. She thought she'd be famous."

Trevor exchanged glances with Maddie. There was no doubt this had been the killer.

"Did she say anything more about this person?" Maddie's voice had an urgent edge to it.

"No." Gretchen shook her head. "That's him, isn't it? The one who killed my sister?"

Instead of answering, Maddie turned to Fred. "I'm going to see if we can track where Mercy was when she sent the text."

"I know she hadn't left the hospital parking lot yet," Gretchen offered.

Trevor quickly sent a discreet text to his lieutenant. Someone needed to check the hospital footage of the parking lot. If they could get a glimpse of the person who approached Mercy, they might have their killer.

It was nearly eight-thirty in the evening by the time they walked out the front door of the Oldens' house.

"I sent a text to my lieutenant. They'll go through the security footage anyway, since the hospital parking lot is a crime scene.," he told her.

"I hope—"

She never finished her sentence. A bullet cracked the driveway where she'd stood less than two seconds earlier. A second shot followed. She cried out then grabbed her gun with her right hand.

"I can't shoot," she whispered to him. "It's too dark and too densely populated here."

Trevor pulled her behind a tree. "It's coming from ahead of us."

The door opened behind them. "Stay inside!" Maddie yelled. The door slammed shut.

He called it in, knowing it would be too late by the time the cops arrived. In the distance, he heard an engine roar to life. Tires squealed. Whoever it was, they'd be long gone within seconds.

"Hopefully, the bullet casings that were dropped will give us a hint."

She didn't say anything. When he looked down, Maddie had collapsed. He felt for a pulse, nearly weeping when he found one. She was breathing, but he could feel the blood seeping through her coat.

He gently laid her down and took off his coat. It took him a moment to find the wound in her shoulder. He put pressure on it.

Someone stood behind him. Jerking back, he looked up to see Gretchen's face. "I called 911. They're on the way."

Chapter Seven

Maddie groaned. Her shoulder was on fire. What had happened?

Her eyes opened. She frowned and tried to sit up. It felt like she was moving in slow motion. The only time she'd ever felt this lethargic had been when she was injured in the line of duty last year and had been given a super powerful medication to dull the pain. The moment she'd realized it had also dulled her reflexes and made her mind hazy, she'd stopped taking it.

"Hey! Careful. You'll rip your stitches."

She turned her head and found Trevor sitting in an uncomfortable looking chair at her bedside.

"Why am I in the hospital again? And what time is it?" Even her voice sounded blurry.

His dark eyes widened. "It's a little after five in the morning. You don't remember going to the Olden house last night?"

She squeezed her eyes tightly closed, trying to force the memories to the front of her brain. Slowly, the painkiller-induced fog cleared. "I remember. The nurse at the hospital, the one who gave the interview, she was murdered. We talked with Mercy's parents."

She grimaced. She'd never enjoy conversations like those. A new memory entered her mind. Her eyes popped wide open. "I was shot! That's why my shoulder hurts so much."

"Yeah. The bullet missed the artery. Otherwise, we might have been in real trouble. I kept pressure on the wound until help arrived. Gretchen brought me two towels from their house to use. You've lost a lot of blood, but you're okay. By the time the ambulance arrived, the bleeding had nearly stopped. The bullet went clean through."

She rested her head back against the pillow. "Two questions. How long do I have to stay, and did you get the shooter?"

"I don't know how long you'll have to stay. And no, I didn't. I couldn't leave you. You would have bled to death if I'd left you. Besides, I think the shooter scrammed almost before you were on the ground. In the dark, I had no visuals to tell where the shots were coming from. I couldn't see anyone."

"Well, maybe we can find the bullets and get a lucky break."

"I doubt the bullets will be in the system."

"Yeah, me too." Discouraged, she closed her eyes again. They kept missing. Would anyone die today because the killer had escaped? "Where's my phone?"

"I have it."

"Did my mom call?"

"She sent a text. I called her this morning and told her you were sleeping. I figured I'd let you decide how much to tell her. She and the girls arrived at your uncle's house. It's on full lockdown, and they are well guarded. The twins were in bed."

"I'm not going to tell her I was shot. Not until this is over. Maybe not even then. There are some things my mother doesn't need to know."

Silence fell between them. She started to drift off to sleep when he spoke again.

"You were amazing," Trevor said.

Her gaze flew to his face. "What?"

"Seriously. When the daughter started talking about how the cops had caused it, I thought you were going to have trouble holding back your opinion. But you handled it smooth as butter."

He shook his head. Maybe she was reading him wrong, but she thought she saw admiration in the look he cast her way.

"It wasn't as hard as you think. I could empathize with her. I remember the night the police knocked on our door and told us about Dad and Nick. Hit and run, they said. I was so angry." She swallowed the lump clogging her throat. The memory hurt even now.

"I recall. I had never felt so helpless." Sorrow drenched his soft voice.

Hearing it, she reached out with her uninjured arm and gripped his hand. "You helped. I don't know what I would have done without you. You let me scream and cry, or rage, and never judged. Even when I yelled at God, you were so steady."

"You would have done the same for me."

It would have sounded trite had anyone else said it. Almost cliché. But from him, it was nothing but the truth.

"Yeah, I would have."

"What happened to us? How did we go from being that close to not talking?" There was no accusation in his question.

She slammed her mouth shut, shame burning in her soul. She knew there was no "we" to that question. It had all been her. She'd shut their friendship down, and even now, she knew she'd made the wrong decision. But it was the only option she could see at the time. Out of all the choices she'd made when she married Alex, shutting out her family and Trevor were the ones she regretted most. To this day, Mom didn't know the full truth, although Maddie imagined her mother had guessed enough.

But Trevor was still in the dark.

He deserved to know the truth. What would he say? Would his admiration survive the realization of how weak and frail she really was?

Did she want to fix them? The answer, she was astonished to discover, was yes. She wanted Trevor back in her life.

But she didn't know if she'd be satisfied with only friendship. Shocked at where her own thoughts were taking her, she bailed. She couldn't talk about this now. "I know we should talk about it. I want to talk about it. Truly. But can this conversation wait? We have so much going on right now."

She didn't want to add that she felt a little too vulnerable to talk about something that nearly destroyed her. Because if she talked about their friendship, she'd have to bring up Alex and admit how she, a cop, had been lulled into an abusive relationship. She still had difficulty accepting that fact. She definitely wasn't keen on talking about it. The counselor she saw after Alex's death told her talking to those she was close to might be cathartic.

Might be. She didn't want to deal with it now.

He sighed, then nodded. "Yeah, it can wait. And you're right. There's a killer we need to track down and put away. But I want you to understand something, Mads. I'm not going to just go away when the case is over. If there's any way I can keep you in my life this time, I plan to do what it takes."

The ice inside melted a bit. Then she shook herself. Lying here thinking about the past wasn't productive. She needed to be doing something. Her uniform was on the table next to the bed. Using her uninjured arm, she shoved the blankets back.

"Trevor, I'm going to change, then I want to see Elaine."

He startled. Then he shrugged. "I guess I should have expected this. You never did like staying in bed even when you were sick."

"Nope. Still don't. There's someone out there blowing things up and shooting people. I need to help stop them."

He paused. "That's what I was thinking."

"Huh?" She paused in the middle of trying to get her feet untangled from the hospital sheet. "What do you mean?"

"Isn't it weird that this killer goes from blowing things up to shooting? What if we're looking for several people?"

She considered it. "It's possible. I won't rule it out."

Trevor stood and strode to the door. "I'll wait for you in the hall. Let's stop by and see if Elaine is awake and talking before we leave. Holler if you need my help."

"Yeah, yeah. I think that's what I just said."

He smirked and left the room, closing the door gently behind him. She waited until she heard the latch click before shooting from the bed, ignoring her shoulder when it protested. She found a mirror and took a quick peek at the injury.

Hmm. Could have been worse. She dressed quickly, fingering the hole in her best uniform shirt before sighing and striding to the door. Such was the price of the job. She needed to get over it and return to work.

Opening the door, she found Trevor leaning against the wall checking his email on his phone. He held up one finger. She waited, watching his expressive face as he typed out a response. Something disturbed him. His brow lowered, and a slight scowl contorted his face.

Why had she never noticed how handsome he was before? When they were teens, he'd merely been her best friend. She laughed when all her girlfriends sighed over Trevor. He was just her oldest pal. No big deal.

Seeing him close up now, she wondered how she'd missed it. Trevor was the whole package. Not only was he good looking, but he was also strong and courageous, compassionate, and had a purity of faith that stunned her. It made her want to remember what being a Christian was like.

Would she ever have a man like that in her own life?

The thought shocked her. Not only because she had deliberately done all she could to keep all men at a distance since the catastrophe that was Alex exited her life, but also because she realized that, for her, there would only ever be one man like Trevor. Her feelings for him had changed, but had he developed stronger feelings for her?

And even if he had, how could she even think of opening her heart again when she had her daughters to protect?

But Trevor wasn't an unknown entity. She knew him.

"Done. You ready?"

Disturbed by the direction her thoughts were flowing, she nodded and kept her eyes away from him as they walked. This case couldn't be solved soon enough. She wouldn't be able to get her equilibrium back until she stood on her own feet without him so close and took a long, objective look at her life.

*

Trevor cast a sidelong glance at the woman walking next to him. Something had happened between the time he left her room and when she had joined him in the hall. Had he done something to offend her? Nothing came to mind. Maybe he was wrong.

Another look her way confirmed it. She wouldn't meet his eyes. The night before, it had seemed that the invisible wall she kept between them had begun to crumble. Now, it was firmly back in place.

Frustrated, he shoved his hands in his coat pocket. He hadn't realized how much he missed having her in his life. Every day with Maddie added a little extra zest.

When she was talking to him, that is.

"They've released Elaine from the ICU." He told her, his voice seeming overly loud in the sterile hallway. "I asked a nurse about her while I waited for you. She's in recovery on the first floor."

"That's fantastic." She met his gaze finally, a relieved smile on her face. "I was really worried about her."

"I know you were." He nearly reached out to pat her shoulder. His brain caught up with his instincts, and he kept his hand in his pocket. She wouldn't appreciate it. Better not take the chance.

They took the elevator down to the first floor. The small space hummed with tension. Trevor wished he knew what had brought it on so he could know what to do to diffuse it. He held in a sigh. Now was not the time to worry about it, but he refused to let her disappear again. His intuition told him her marriage had been the root of their severed relationship. He could understand a man not wanting his wife to have a male best friend. When he'd been dating Angie, she'd made quite a few snarky comments about his friendship with Maddie. Back then, he had scoffed and brushed them off. Although he and Angie dated for almost a year, he'd never thought about their lives beyond college. The idea of ending his friendship with Maddie hadn't come up. Angie's attitude had made for a few strained situations, though. If she'd lived, and if they had gotten married, would she have forced the issue? As an adult, he could see where having a female best friend might not have gone over well.

Still. The way she'd dropped him without a word or explanation, that was not the way Maddie would have handled it. Something else was up. He'd have to bide his time to find out. But he wouldn't rest until he gave their friendship his best shot.

Would friendship be enough? Given her attitude, it had to be. He rubbed his chest, trying to soothe away the ache in his heart.

He hadn't had a serious relationship since Angie died. Between her death and the pain of Maddie's desertion, he'd had enough heartache. Would he be willing to risk it again? He shoved the thought away.

The elevator bumped to a halt, and the door whooshed open. They stepped into the hall. An officer lay on the ground, his skin waxy.

Trevor threw Maddie a startled glance, then they raced to the room. "Check on Elaine!"

Trevor dropped down beside the officer. He knew without touching him that the man was dead. He was a new officer. Only on the force for six months. Trevor didn't even know his name. A fact that shamed him.

"Call a doctor!" Maddie yelled. "I think she's been poisoned."

Why poison? He knew as soon as he thought it. Guns were noisy. The killer needed to be able to leave without getting caught. He saw a tiny drop of dried blood on the officer's neck. Probably caused by a needle. When the coroner's report came back, Trevor felt certain poison would be the reason for his death.

He yanked out his phone and made the call. Within moments, the empty hall swarmed with police, doctors and hospital staff. Chief Kennedy approached him. Sorrow had carved deep lines on either side of his mouth.

Trevor suddenly realized that this was the first officer the LaMar Pond Police Department had lost since Irene Kennedy's first husband, Tony Martello, had died in the line of duty seven years earlier. It never got easier.

"How's Elaine?" Chief Kennedy asked.

Maddie stepped into the hall next to them. "She's going to be fine, Chief. She's mad. A woman entered the room dressed as a nurse and tried to give her a shot. She was suspicious and fought it so most of the poison spilled. Only a little bit got under her skin. She's been given an antidote."

"I saw some blood on Rob's neck. I'll bet he was jabbed from behind after letting the nurse into the room." Trevor reported.

They were all silent thinking of the dead officer. The chief sighed. "Poor Rob. He was a good man. I don't look forward to calling his parents and telling them what happened."

Maddie winced. No doubt remembering a similar experience she had had the night before. "Chief?"

"Yes, Sergeant?"

"Elaine can't identify the woman who poisoned her. She wore a mask. But she got a good view of the bomber. She will be released either today or tomorrow. But either way, she wants to get working on a sketch immediately to get his image out there to all the surrounding precincts."

The chief straightened. "That is something. I'll make sure it happens today."

When the doctor asked them to step out, Chief Kennedy motioned for the team to leave. He quietly asked one of the other officers to remain on guard. "We'll be in the waiting room."

Nearly an hour later, a doctor approached. "Chief Kennedy, the officer's family has arrived."

Chief Kennedy sighed and followed him. Trevor mentally offered a prayer for the chief and the family of the fallen man. Only God could help in times like this.

It was several hours before they were able to leave. He'd got Maddie and himself some breakfast sandwiches and coffee from the café. She'd grimaced after her first sip, and he couldn't blame her. The coffee was watered down and lukewarm. Even the sugar she added didn't appear to improve her enjoyment.

"You won't hurt my feelings if you don't drink it," he informed her.

She snorted. "I'm not concerned about your feelings, Trev. I need caffeine. I feel ready to fall over."

He laughed, but a new spark of hope lit inside him. She hadn't called him Trev in years. That little nickname might not have seemed important, but to him it was a sign that she hadn't been as successful at distancing herself as he feared.

She finished her coffee and dropped the cup in the garbage. "I'm going back to see Elaine. Then can we go to my place? I want to pack a bag and call my mom."

"Sure."

"Elaine." Maddie greeted her partner when they entered the room. "You okay if I leave?"

"I am. But you should see the image of the bomber before you go."

Maddie whistled. "You found him? Already? That was quick."

"I'm not happy about it," Elaine said, her eyes serious. "He was in the database. Maddie, he was a cop once."

Trevor halted so fast, she bumped into him. "Was he on the bomb squad?"

Elaine's eyes widened. "He was. Do you know him?"

"If it's who I think it is, then yes. I know him. I'm also the reason he was kicked off the squad."

Chapter Eight

Trevor held onto the shred of hope that the bomber wasn't Keith White, that it was all a coincidence. So much time had gone by since he'd last seen him, he'd nearly forgotten that remote triggers were Keith's favorite kind. He had always enjoyed playing around with explosives and had been a highly skilled member of the team. But his other issues outshined his positive points.

Maybe it wasn't him.

The moment he saw the image of his former colleague staring back at him, that hope slid away, and despair threatened to take its place.

It wasn't his fault. Mentally, he knew it. But still, he couldn't rid himself of the guilt. If only...

If only what? He hadn't had any choice. If the same situation happened today, he'd act the same way. Yet still, he couldn't drag his mind away from the memories.

"Do you want to tell me about it?"

He turned his head and watched Maddie buckle herself into his truck. This time, Misty wasn't sitting in back. He'd gone home last night after Maddie had been admitted and taken care of the dog. It would have been cruel to leave her in the truck for so long. At least at home, she had a dog door to let herself out and the run of his yard.

"I haven't seen or heard from Keith in fifteen years," He mused. "Not since we were fresh out of the academy."

"I never met him."

"Well, no. You were a couple years behind us because you went to college."

She shrugged. "I thought I wanted to be a teacher. It wasn't until I actually started taking education classes that I discovered it wasn't my passion."

"I know." He took a swig from the bottle of Mountain Dew he'd bought before they left. "Anyway, Keith and I were never close, but I didn't dislike the guy. He was a bit too arrogant for me. Overconfident. I've thought over what happened a million times. I don't think I could have acted any differently."

"Trevor, what happened?"

"Keith took risks. He didn't follow protocol, and he ignored orders. And someone died because of it. He took a shortcut, and a bomb went off. There was a civilian casualty, and our commander ended up in the hospital, unconscious."

"How awful!"

"It was. But then he tried to blackmail me into lying about the orders we were given. In his mind, it was perfectly acceptable to let our commander take the rap for what he did."

"Obviously, you didn't do that."

He let out a slow breath at the strength of her confidence in him.

"I didn't. They came down hard on him. He lost his commission and his badge. No second chances. The commander woke up a few days later. He was enraged at Keith's attempt to sully his reputation." He paused. "I wonder, seeing him, if this was part of a plan to take vengeance on me."

She shook her head. "I think it's deeper than that. It's possible, as you said, that we have two people working together. I don't know if your role in his termination comes into play here. Probably he's out to get the department at large. Or maybe he has some other motivation. We just don't know what yet."

"I get what you're saying." He rubbed a hand down the side of his face. It wasn't comfortable, being this vulnerable, but he'd already gone so far. "I can't help wondering if there was something I could have done. I don't regret what happened with Keith. That was his choice. I do regret that someone died. If I had seen the red flags earlier, maybe I could have prevented that."

A harsh laugh escaped from her. "You have those thoughts, too?"

He slid his gaze her way briefly. "You, too?"

For a moment, he thought she'd refuse to answer. Or change the subject. Finally, she made a strange growling sound.

"I regret letting a man I barely knew fool me with his smooth-talking ways. He nearly cost me everything."

"If you want to talk…" he extended the same offer to her that she'd given him earlier.

"I don't." She shook her head. "At the same time, I do. And I admit, you kind of deserve to know what happened."

He didn't dare make a sound. Finally, after all these years, he'd learn the truth. But he dreaded it, knowing that he'd hear about her suffering. Suffering she hadn't trusted him with before. He kept his face blank. She had always teased him about how easily his emotions were to read. What she never seemed to understand was his deepest emotions all involved her.

*

Could she do it? Could she tell him the truth about Alex?

She opened and closed her mouth a couple of times before she finally got the courage to speak. But she had to. These past two days, she'd remembered what their friendship had meant to her. Had their roles been switched and he'd cut her off without a word, it would have crushed her.

She owed him the truth, no matter how late it was in coming. Taking a deep breath, she braced herself. "You already know I went to college and met Alex, my ex-husband. Or should I call him my late husband? He's both."

He shook his head. "I wasn't aware that he died, but yeah. I'd heard you'd gotten married. That's all I know."

She bit her lip. How did she start? "I'm not going to tell you every minute detail. What's important was that I met him, and we married after knowing each other only about six months. It seemed romantic at the time. Now, I can't believe I did that."

"That does seem impulsive."

She heard the careful phrasing. "Even for me, right?"

When he opened his mouth, she waved it away. "You're right, of course. The first few months were great. I never noticed then how manipulative he was. I got pregnant almost immediately. And as soon as we knew I was expecting twins, his insistence that working full time would be too difficult made sense. The doctor had told us that it was a high-risk pregnancy."

She frowned. "But then, he started tearing me down, piece by piece. He'd get jealous if I spent too much time with anyone other than him. When I told him I planned to go home and see my mom one weekend, I made the mistake of mentioning visiting you. He hit the roof. It terrified me."

Trevor's hands tightened on the steering wheel. "Did he hit you?"

"Not then."

His knuckles stood out, stark white. She knew he'd understood what she meant. Quickly she hurried on, desperate to finish the distasteful story of her ignorance. "I still don't know how it happened. He managed to separate me from all my friends and from my mom. When I went into labor early, I had no one but him by my side."

She took a drink of her water. It was warm now. "In the hospital, one of the nurses tried to counsel me about emotional abuse. I scoffed at her and told her she was delusional, that my marriage was fine. But I knew it wasn't. I was scared though. I had no one, I thought. And he controlled everything. I didn't have a job, and now I had two babies who required lots of care. He made comments about how if we ever separated, he'd get custody because I wouldn't be able to care for them without him."

"He knew you were thinking of leaving. Even if you didn't."

"Either that, or he was making sure I wouldn't."

There was a brief, heavy silence. "Maddie, what changed?"

"What you think. He finally got physically aggressive." That was easier to say than to say that he hit her. Trevor bowed his head. "It happened one time. The twins were sleeping in their crib two feet away from me. I thought, what if he hits them? Two days later, he went to work, taking the only car. I went to the neighbor and begged for help. By the time he got home, I was gone, holed up at my mother's house. He showed up, yelling and threatening, and we got it on video. That was enough for a restraining order. I filed for divorce. He died almost two years later. He'd been in a car accident. A car accident he'd caused by road rage. It was just a few weeks before the twins turned two. They didn't know him. I had a court order giving me complete control. I left my mother's house and moved away. He still managed to find my phone number. His mother started calling me and ranting about how it was my fault and she'd see I paid and lose the kids. But I blocked her.

Then I went to the phone company and changed my phone number, again. When the courts denied her petition for custody of the kids, I moved back in with my mom and we started over."

"Maddie. Could your mother-in-law be involved in all this?"

She shook her head. "Nah. She died of alcohol poisoning a couple of years ago. That's when I could finally breathe freely. I bought a house, but made sure I stayed near Mom. I wouldn't make the mistake of pushing her away again."

He turned into her driveway and shifted the truck into Park but didn't get out. "Maddie, why didn't you ever call me? You've been back in LaMar Pond for years. Until yesterday, we haven't said more than a few words to each other. Surely, you didn't think I'd blame you?"

She blinked back the tears. His face, so familiar, blurred. "I didn't know what to tell you. I was embarrassed and ashamed. And," she ducked her head, "I no longer trusted my judgment about men. I have no male friends. Haven't gone out socially with any men, even as friends, since I came back."

"He destroyed your trust in me." His voice had deepened. She heard the rough anger under the smooth tones. "It will be hard to forgive him for that. I have to, though. He's dead, and anger won't help anyone."

"It took me a long time to understand that. But I do regret letting what he did to me continue to impact my life."

He turned to face her completely, fusing his gaze with hers. The intensity in his stare made her falter. She looked away and recalled why they were at her house. "I need to go get a few things together. I'll be back in a moment."

"What if he's here?"

She stopped two steps from the truck. He'd been so supportive. It wouldn't hurt her to humor him. Coming back to the passenger side door, she grabbed her water.

"I'll be careful once I go in, but let's be sure my porch isn't rigged, shall we?" She sent him a sassy grin and then casually lobbed the plastic bottle toward her porch. It hit the wooden deck with a thud and rolled toward the top step.

She lifted her eyebrows at Trevor. "Are you satis—"

The porch exploded. The force of it sent her crashing into Trevor, smashing them against the side of the truck.

Chapter Nine

If she hadn't listened to Trevor's concerns, she'd be dead right now. Lifting her head, she stared at the front of her home. The beautiful porch was burning, and pillars that had held the roof up had been blown to smithereens. The roof had collapsed and lay smoldering where she would have stood.

She shivered.

Trevor took out his cell phone. She listened as he called dispatch. Hearing the destruction of her home described, she shook. Trevor came closer and slung an arm around her shoulders, supporting her while talking with the dispatcher. Maddie burrowed into him, turning her face into his shoulder. Once, she thought he kissed her hair, but it seemed unlikely.

Trevor's arms tightened around her. She'd been so shocked by the explosion, she hadn't even noticed that he was holding her.

"Are you hurt?"

She shook her head. "No. That was too close."

"We have to call this in. Then let's go to my place and grab Misty."

All she wanted was a nap. That would have to wait. "I was the intended target yesterday, wasn't I?"

"I think so."

"Why? We haven't hung around together for years." She narrowed her eyes and took in her damaged home again. "You've never been here before today. I don't understand why he'd target me."

Trevor let his arms drop away when she moved out of reach. He shoved a hand through his short dark blonde hair, making it stand up in places. Normally she'd smile at the sight. Today, seeing him flustered just emphasized how desperate the situation had become.

"If I had to guess, I'd say he's taken some time to gather information about me. He'd know we used to be friends. I talked about you all the time. I doubt he knows we haven't spoken."

She blushed.

Trevor continued. "Who else would he go after? My parents are in Florida. I have no other family. And Keith always treated the women in the field as if they were weak and didn't really deserve to be part of the team. I think he's a bit of a coward. Of course, he wouldn't go after me directly or one of my buddies."

Maddie pursed her lips. "So, I'm the weak link?"

If she had met Keith while he was still in the field, she probably wouldn't have liked him. Guys like him gave the uniform a bad rep.

"No. But he'd think you are. He has no idea what a force you are."

The pleasure of hearing what he thought of her warmed her frozen soul.

"Why now, though? He's had years to get his revenge."

"No idea. That's one thing we'll ask him when we get him."

She scrunched her nose at him.

"Don't give me that look. We have a name and a description. This is a person many of the cops and bomb squad members, not to mention the firefighters and EMTs, know and have a history with. He didn't plan very well. If he had, he'd have disguised his appearance."

"Yeah, that's true."

"And," he added, dragging out the word for emphasis, "it wouldn't surprise me to discover he's been working with the security company that contracted with the school. He's so overconfident, he's not even bothering to cover his tracks. His arrogance will be his downfall."

She loved his optimism. It was contagious. Hopefully, his confidence would be rewarded.

By the time the police, the bomb squad and the fire department arrived, she had her emotions tightly in control. Exhausted, hungry and thirsty, she did her best to ignore the signals her body sent her brain. Someone blew up her home. The place where she and her daughters lived and expected to be safe and secure.

Would she ever feel safe again?

"Maddie, here." Lily Shepherd marched up to her and held out a bottle of water, a peanut butter and jelly sandwich and an apple.

"What's this?" She accepted the food, grateful but confused. Her stomach rumbled loudly. She took a bite of the apple, humming as the sweet and tangy juice hit her taste buds.

Lily jerked a thumb over her shoulder to where Trevor stood, conferring with his team. "Trevor Stone called me a few minutes ago and asked me to bring you some food. Said you hadn't eaten since yesterday."

"All true." She took a bite of the sandwich. She didn't care how childish it seemed. Nothing satisfied her hunger like soft bread and creamy peanut butter. "I appreciate this."

Lily lifted one shoulder in an elegant shrug. "We had it all in the kitchen at the station."

Maddie didn't care where it came from. She was touched, both by Trevor's thoughtfulness and her colleague's taking the time to fix her a simple meal. It was little acts like this that kept her from feeling completely alone.

She recalled the way Trevor had prayed for her the night before. She still got shot. Her shoulder continued to ache each time she moved her arm. Despite that, and despite the sheer agony of watching emergency personnel tromp around what was left of her house trying to stop the fire that continued to blaze and make sure there were no other explosives, she had a sense of being watched over.

"Sergeant!" She twisted around at the call.

Chief Kennedy walked quickly in her direction.

"Yes, chief?"

"First, are you sure you're all right? You've had a rough twenty-four hours."

"Fine, sir. But when this is over, I'm going to need a vacation."

He didn't laugh. Didn't even crack a smile. "We'll find him, Maddie. Everyone in the department wants in on this case."

She nodded, the knot in her throat making speech momentarily impossible. Clearing her throat twice, she managed to speak around it. "Thank you, sir. I appreciate it."

"Chief!" a young officer ran up to him. "We have something."

The chief motioned for him to lead the way. When he followed the officer, Maddie ran after him. Hopefully, whatever they found would help them locate Keith.

*

Trevor squatted close to the ground, his gaze following the footprints in the dirt.

"Trevor, what do you have?" Chief Kennedy stomped to a halt a foot from him, Maddie at his shoulder. Trevor kept his attention on the chief. He was hyper aware of Maddie's presence, but his focus remained on the job. That was the best way to help her reclaim her life.

And if things worked out the way he prayed they would, he'd be in that life with her. Whether he was kept as a friend or allowed the privilege of one day becoming more, he didn't know. His heart squeezed. After all this, he knew it was possible he'd be shunted to the side again.

He'd cope.

But not before he did his best to make his way back to her side where he belonged.

"Sir," he addressed the chief. "I believe the bomber stood here and watched us when Maddie and I arrived. You can see the footprints, still fresh and undisturbed."

"Why didn't he use a remote detonator again?" Maddie asked. "I thought you said that was his favorite kind."

"I think when we investigate, we'll find it was by remote. You took a step toward the porch. He probably hit the switch, and during the delay, you turned back to me. Had you not stopped, you would have been killed." He spoke matter-of-factly, but inside, he felt like he might lose the small bit of food he'd eaten.

At his side, Maddie shuddered.

The chief squatted near him. "Indeed. Looks like two sets of prints."

Trevor pointed at the second set. "Yeah. Maddie and I wondered if it was one culprit or two. If I had to guess, I'd say the second set—"

"Is female," Maddie whispered, her narrowed gaze zeroed in on the smaller impressions.

"I think so." The second set of prints were narrower, smaller and had a more defined heel. As if the person was wearing dress boots with a chunky heel. And they weren't as deep as the prints he believed to be Keith's.

"I'll bet this lady, whoever she is, is good with a gun."

Maddie's gaze shot to his. "So, he set the bombs..."

"But she's the one who shot Mercy. We just found this." He held up his hand. In it he held an evidence bag. A single syringe was enclosed in it. "I can't promise, but I bet when this is examined, it will have the same poison used on Elaine and Rob."

"They tried to keep Elaine and Mercy from identifying the bomber, but they failed." Maddie murmured. "There's nothing I want more than to make sure the guy- or the people- responsible are caught and are sentenced to life in prison. It won't bring Rob or Mercy back, but it might give their families some small sense of closure."

They didn't have time to consider it too long.

It took five hours to deal with the fire and find the explosive set under the porch. It was a remote detonator, just as he'd expected. The acid in his stomach roiled at the find.

If Maddie hadn't turned back...

He stood and briskly strode away from the site. He couldn't breathe right. Sucking in a huge breath, he held it in his lungs, desperate to calm his racing heart. When she broke off their friendship, it had been hard. He'd been angry and bitter for a long time. He felt like she'd thrown him over, like he meant nothing.

Even when he walked around feeling like his heart had been yanked out, he didn't put two and two together. He'd always assumed he'd been so angry because his best friend had dropped him. When she returned to LaMar Pond, he'd avoided her and nursed his anger until God convicted him that he needed to forgive her. Still, he attributed all those emotions to a broken friendship.

How could he not have seen it?

When she'd been shot, he'd have traded places with her in an instant. He didn't leave her side for longer than absolutely necessary. He knew he was on thin ice then.

But when he heard her tell him about her husband, the fury roiling in his gut told him he was sunk.

Whatever happened, he was completely in love with Madalyn Blake. And probably always had been.

Would she ever love him back?

First things first. He needed to keep her alive and find the killers.

He couldn't believe Keith would come after him after all this time. But Trevor had learned to trust his gut. It had proven to be reliable in the past. Keith had been an angry, belligerent man when they'd met years ago. It stood to reason that if he hadn't found a productive outlet for his grief and anger, it would have festered. By this time, no doubt he'd convinced himself that rather than doing his job, that Trevor was in the wrong. Keith had become a narcissist, unwilling or unable to see his own part in his problems. Trevor recalled the incident that had led to Keith's downfall. Not only had an innocent died because of his carelessness, but Keith had felt no compunction about plotting to ruin a fellow officer's career to keep his own nose clean.

No. There were things Trevor regretted in his life, sure. Getting Keith kicked off the bomb squad was not one of them.

"Trevor?"

Her voice pierced him. He braced himself and tried to keep his expression flat. Maddie had often told him his face gave away what he thought. But not always. He'd trained himself to keep his thoughts hidden when it mattered. Like now.

Rotating on his heel, he came face to face with her. She looked like she'd fall down at any moment.

"Your lieutenant said we're done."

"Great. Let's get back to my place. We can clean up, feed Misty and plan our next move."

The firetrucks departed first. Immediately after, the other vehicles began to pull out, until only Trevor, Maddie and Officer Shepherd remained. The other officer got into her cruiser and started it up. Trevor opened the passenger door of his truck for Maddie and stood aside so she could enter.

She placed one hand on the door and moved to enter.

Smash!

The window shattered, scattering shards of glass around her feet.

There was a sniper in the trees!

Chapter Ten

"**M**addie! Get down!"

Trevor ducked behind the door next to her. A second shot rang out and slammed against the door. Trevor slipped his own weapon from its holster. At his elbow, Maddie had her Glock ready.

"Where are the shots coming from?"

He inched toward the edge of the door and glanced around. "I don't see anyone. My guess is behind those trees."

"If we leave the door open to shield us, we might be able to crawl around to the other side."

He nodded. "Move carefully and stay low."

She gave him a "Really?" look. If the situation weren't so precarious, he would have smiled. Maddie had always despised when he took a patronizing tone. As a teenager, he sometimes did it just to annoy her. At the moment, his only goal was to get them both out of this. Alive.

Carefully, keeping their bodies pressed against the length of the truck, they edged along the side toward the back. The sniper must have been aware of their movements. Several shots in quick succession burst through the tree cover and sprayed the front passenger side of the truck.

As Trevor speculated, the shots didn't touch them.

She was at the wrong angle.

A shot rang out behind them. Officer Shepherd had opened fire on the sniper. Her aim was true. An enraged howl followed the shot.

"I think Lily got her," Maddie said. "She was a sniper, you know."

He hadn't known that. But for her to take a shot like that and hit the target, it wasn't hard to believe. He grabbed his phone and dialed the dispatcher again. "We have a sniper in the trees. Multiple shots have been fired. Officer Shepherd may have struck the sniper."

"Good shot." Maddie murmured to her colleague. "Hopefully you hit her gun hand so she can't shoot anymore."

Judging by the yell, she wasn't dead. Additionally, it was definitely a woman shouting. "Maddie. Did you recognize her voice when she yelled? Was it someone you knew?"

"I'm not sure. Most people don't go around yelling so it was hard to tell if it was a voice I recognize."

Backup arrived within minutes. The police hadn't had a chance to get very far away before the shooting started. The officers put on their protective gear before heading towards the woods in the general direction of where the shooting originated. Trevor, Maddie and Lily joined them.

Trevor had the desire to place himself ahead of Maddie. It was a challenge to see her moving away from him. He knew she was trained to handle situations like this, the same as he and all the other law enforcement officers were. Still, seeing the woman he loved marching toward where a known sniper had been and not being able to protect her went against his instincts.

He forced himself to continue. Maddie was more than competent.

Up ahead to the left, there was a shout. All the officers converged on the spot.

"There's a trail of blood. It's fresh."

Officer Shepherd had hit the target. It was impossible to see how injured the sniper had been. The blood was difficult to follow by itself. Fortunately, a pair of distinct footprints went along with the blood spatter. The prints were the same that Trevor had found earlier at the explosion site.

"It looks like our sniper is a woman." He pointed to the prints. "I don't know how fast she can travel between those heels and the injury."

"I wouldn't count on the heels slowing her down." Maddie scanned the horizon, searching for any signs of movement. "If it's her natural choice of footwear, she's probably used to moving in them. Plus, chunky heels aren't that hard to maneuver in."

He squinted at her. "Really?"

She rolled her shoulders, wincing. He'd nearly forgotten about her injury. "Yeah. I don't care for them, but I've seen a woman running in heels before."

Lily snorted. "Me, too. I'd fall flat on my face if I tried that. But it can be done."

They followed the prints until they ended abruptly.

Maddie swept a hand to indicate tire tracks. "Her car must have been parked here."

Chief Kennedy called the hospital, asking them to report any possible gunshot victims directly to him.

"Do you think she'll go to the hospital?" Skepticism colored Maddie's tone.

"No, I don't. But I don't want to overlook the possibility." He looked at Maddie. "You two are due for some rest. We'll keep you updated, but you're relieved of duty for now. We have to get what evidence is here logged."

"Come on, Maddie. We'll only be two more people possibly messing up any evidence."

It was a sign of how exhausted Maddie was that she didn't argue. She stumbled beside him as they returned to his trunk. He checked the passenger seat to make sure she wouldn't be sitting on broken glass, then she got in and buckled her seatbelt. He shut the door and jogged around to the driver's side.

Glancing over at the woman beside him, he noticed her eyes had closed. He refrained from speaking on the short drive to his house. By the time they arrived, her slowed breathing informed him she was out completely. He hated to wake her but knew she couldn't sleep in the truck. It was chilly with the window broken.

Gently, he called her name. When she didn't respond, he called louder. She stirred. "Come on, Maddie. We're here."

She nodded, rubbing her eyes like a child. He hid a smile, amused for the first time since she was shot.

Misty met them at the door, her long tail waving ecstatically. "Okay, girl. I'll take care of you. Just give me a minute."

Leading her down a hall to the spare bedroom he usually reserved for his parents when they visited, he turned on the light inside the door. "The bathroom's next door if you need to clean up. Help yourself to anything. There's plenty of food in the fridge."

She nodded, then disappeared into the bathroom.

He called Misty, then left Maddie to her own devices while he fed the dog and contacted a buddy to see about getting his window repaired. The next time he ventured past the guest room, the door was closed, and he could hear Maddie moving around inside.

"Everything all right?" he called. "Do you need anything?"

"I'm good." She responded. Her voice broke off in a yawn. "I'm going to sleep for a while."

"I'll wake you if anything happens."

It felt strange moving about his place, knowing she was there. But strange in a good way. He should take the opportunity to rest up, as well. He picked up a blanket and turned on the television. He'd lie on the couch for a while.

Ten minutes later, he turned off the television and stood. As exhausted as he was, there was no way he could sleep. He had too much going through his brain. If Maddie hadn't been sleeping in the back room, he'd take Misty and go for a run to work off some of his stress. He did some of his best thinking that way.

There was no way he'd leave her unattended. Not after the events of the past two days. He settled for cleaning the kitchen instead. Not as satisfying, but it kept him busy.

His phone rang two hours later. Maddie walked into the kitchen while he was talking. As easily as if she stayed in his house every day, she went to the refrigerator and pulled out a bottle of water and the block of cheddar cheese he'd bought two days ago.

It pleased him to see her so comfortable in his space. It reminded him of the way they'd been as teenagers. They'd always treated each other's homes as if they lived there.

When she lifted the cheese to silently ask if he wanted some, he shook his head.

"That was the chief," he said after he disconnected the call. "They are done at your place. They lost the trail but will let us know if anything else turns up. Also, some good news. Elaine is being released this afternoon. She'll be off duty for a few days, but she'll be fine."

Maddie sighed. The tightness in her shoulders eased. "That is good news. I was really worried about her."

His phone rang again before he could respond. He frowned. "Hey. It's your mom."

"She's probably calling you because my phone is dead," Maddie stated, but her voice was strained.

He accepted the call and put it on speaker. "Hello, Amanda—"

"Trevor! Why didn't you call me? What's going on?" the woman shrieked.

"What do you mean?"

"I got a call that my daughter was hurt when her house exploded!"

*

Maddie heard the tears thickening her mother's voice. "Mom! I'm fine. I'm at Trevor's. Are you driving?"

"Maddie? I don't understand." Amanda's voice remained shaky, but she calmed upon hearing her daughter. "I got a call early this morning, saying your house exploded and you were inside. I left the girls with my brother and headed home immediately. I'll be in LaMar Pond in twenty minutes. I tried your phone, because I couldn't just accept a stranger's word. I called the hospital, they said you'd been released. I tried to call your chief but couldn't get through. I was too frazzled to leave a message."

"I'm okay. I was in the hospital. There was an, um, accident last night." She couldn't tell her mom she'd been shot over the phone. "I'm fine. I don't have time to go into it now, but I will tell you when I see you. Mom, be careful. Someone did put a bomb on my porch, but I wasn't hurt by it."

Trevor put a hand on her arm. "Amanda, go to the police station. I think whoever planted that bomb called you. They must have called you before it even went off."

A shiver of fear raced through Maddie's system. "Mom, listen to him. They may have targeted you."

"I am heading there now. I'm on Sassafras, and I'll be on Main Street in a mile."

"Good. That's only ten minutes from the station." With her mom safe at the station, she wouldn't worry. "Call Uncle Joe and tell him what happened as soon as you're safe. He'll protect the twins."

"I will." There was a pause. "What is this lady doing? She's going to hurt someone with the way she's driving."

"Mom?" Maddie grabbed the phone from Trevor. "Don't stop for anyone! An unknown woman is a suspect. Mom!"

"I hear you. I will... She's got a gun!"

Maddie yelled for her mom. There was a gunshot. Her mother's scream was cut off by the sound of a crash. "Mom! Mom!"

The call ended.

*

Maddie and Trevor raced to the truck. He was already on the phone with dispatch and sending help to her mother's location. Maddie jumped inside the cab and slammed the door. She drummed her fingers on the door while she waited for Trevor to start the vehicle. It felt like everything was moving in slow motion.

After what felt like an hour, but was only a couple of minutes, they were on their way. Trevor pushed the emergency light onto his dashboard as close to his window as it would go and turned on the siren he'd had installed on his truck. The traffic pulled to the side for them as they barreled past.

Not fast enough. Her mother had been shot at. Was she hurt?

Maddie blocked out the thoughts and fear clogging her mind. Her mother had to be all right. Without pausing to think about what she was doing, Maddie prayed. It was the first time in years she'd prayed on her own. She couldn't formulate any fancy words, just a raw cry for help from the depths of her soul.

They arrived at the scene at the same time as the ambulance was pulling in from the opposite direction. Maddie hopped down from the truck and ran to her mother's car. It was smashed against a tree along the side of the road.

There was so much blood.

The paramedics beat her there.

"Vitals are strong."

She nearly wilted where she stood.

"That leg's broken. Let's move her carefully."

Maddie felt Trevor's arm creep around her shoulder. He kissed her head. "I'm going to assist with traffic control."

She nodded. When more emergency vehicles pulled in, she backed away from the scene, keeping her eyes glued to the car.

A hand grabbed her and yanked her off her feet. She cried out as pain shot up her shoulder. Spinning around, she came face to face with Keith. A sting in her side was the only warning before she lost consciousness.

*

It was dark. Maddie lifted her head. Where was she? Frowning, she glanced around. She was in a dimly lit room lying on a dirty floor.

Sitting up, she stifled a groan.

"So you're awake."

She turned her head. "I don't know you."

Keith smiled urbanely at her. "No. But I know you. You are my ticket for revenge. Trevor Stone destroyed my life. Now I'm going to kill the woman he loves."

She wanted to tell him he was wrong. But she didn't want to aggravate the man. He had a gun pointed right at her.

And she was suddenly aware that if she died here and now, she would have wasted the opportunity to tell Trevor how wrong she'd been. That she did love him. Deeply, in a way she'd never loved Alex. She'd been such a fool.

Now it was too late.

And she'd never see her little girls again.

She didn't dare call attention to their existence. Keith, and whoever his partner was, had already gone after her mother. Her throat threatened to close at the memory of her mom's bloody form stuck in the car. The paramedics said her vitals were strong. Her mom would pull through.

Maddie had no illusions about her own fate. She was alone without a gun, and her mind was still a little hazy from whatever drug he shot her with. This would be, she believed, the day she died. If she had to die to keep all those she loved safe, she would gladly do so.

At least she'd made her peace with God.

"What? No pleading for your life? I'm disappointed."

She shivered. Why was she still alive?

A door opened, and heels clicked across the floor. She raised her eyes as a tall woman came into view. Her jaw dropped. "Danielle?"

Danielle Grant, Alex's sneering younger sister, glared down at her.

"Madalyn." There was so much hate in that one word. "You have more lives than a cat."

"I don't understand."

The other woman rolled her eyes. "You never were too bright. Leaving my brother was the only smart thing you ever did. Of course, I took him out. He always was a thorn in my side."

"Wait. You killed Alex?" She could barely wrap her mind around it.

"Yes." She raised her gun. "I've been waiting to get to you for years. I'd even researched everything I could about your current job. When I learned about your old pal Trevor and how he'd ousted a comrade, I knew I'd found someone who could help me. I was right. Keith was only too willing to help me and get his own revenge. And now I'll take care of you. Poor little girls. They'll have no one. No one but their dear

Aunt Danielle. Thank you, Madalyn. You'll be gone, and I will finally be a mother."

Bile churned at the thought of her twins being at the mercy of this monster. Maddie struggled to rise. Danielle's finger was on the trigger—

Crack. The gun flew from Danielle's hand. She screamed, clutching her hand, blood dripping on the floor.

Maddie glanced over in time to see Chief Kennedy, his service weapon drawn and aimed directly at Danielle. He moved farther into the room, the gun never wavering. And behind him...

"Trevor!"

And then she was in his arms, her head buried in his shoulder.

She ignored the commotion as Danielle and Keith were read their rights and led out of the room. "How did you find me?"

"A witness saw the car she was driving. We were able to track her."

"Five more minutes..."

"Shhh. It's over. Your mom is at the hospital. She'll be fine. And I called and checked on Paige and Piper. They're safe."

His hand drifted down the side of her face. "I almost lost you again."

She lifted her eyes to his and inhaled deeply. His emotions were plain to see.

"You love me," she blurted out. How had she missed it?

He chuckled. "I should have known. I don't even get to make my own declaration."

She was too happy to feel embarrassed at her impulsive outburst. Instead, she snuggled closer. "It's okay. I'll let you make mine for me."

He searched her eyes, hope kindling in his gaze. "You love me, back."

"I do. I can't believe I didn't see it before."

He lowered his forehead to hers. "We were both a little slow to see it. Maybe because we were friends for so long." He paused. "You know, I think our future is looking bright right now."

She laughed. "Already talking about the future."

"You are my future."

He leaned in and caressed her lips with his. When he backed away, she grinned up at him. "Care for seconds?"

He smiled and kissed her again, sealing their love with a silent promise to cherish her always. She'd never again let him drift out of her life. In her mind, she could imagine their lives merging. Her daughters would finally have the father they deserved. And she would have a man who accepted her and supported her. The man who had known her and loved her most of her life. Her best friend and the love of her life all in one.

She smiled and snuggled deeper into his embrace, excited for all the tomorrows they'd have together.

Epilogue

Maddie shut the door of her SUV with her hip because her arms were full. Holding the plastic grocery bags by the handles, she marched up the driveway to the front door of the house, humming. Trevor met her at the front door and held it open for her.

"Let me take those from you, Mads."

"Pay the toll first." She puckered her lips, trying not to laugh.

He grinned and leaned in to kiss her. Bubbles of electricity zipped through her. When he lifted his head, his brown eyes glittered warmly down at her. He held out his hands, and she transferred the bags to him. She removed the light flannel shirt and slipped off her shoes.

"How's the painting coming along?"

They moved to the kitchen and began putting the groceries away together. She loved the spaciousness of the room. When they'd built this house during their engagement, they had hashed out everything they wanted in their forever home. The building itself had been completed two months before their wedding six months ago. They still had a couple of rooms to paint but had decided to wait until the weather warmed and the snow melted so they could leave the windows open and properly ventilate.

"I finished your mom's room. The twins are still debating whether they want pink with light green trim or the other way around."

She grinned. That sounded about right. "Why don't we suggest two walls pink and two walls green?"

He paused with the peanut butter in his hand and turned away from the cupboard. "You know, that just might work for them."

"If they want it redone in a few years, that will be easy enough."

He put the peanut butter and the canned goods away. When he finished, he came over and slid his arms around her from behind. He kissed the top of her head. "Have I told you today how much I love you?"

Sighing, she leaned her back against his chest. "It's been a long time. At least two hours."

"Well, Mrs. Stone, let me correct that. I love you."

She turned in his arms and put her hands around his neck, interlacing her fingers. "Marrying you was the best decision of my life."

She met his lips halfway. She could have stayed like that for hours, standing with the sunlight streaming in the windows, kissing her handsome husband in the middle of their new kitchen. But it wasn't to be.

Giggles exploded behind her. Grinning, she broke away from Trevor and turned her head.

Paige and Piper stood together, splotches of blue paint dotting their paint shirts. Amanda had a hand on both girls' shoulders. "Now girls, why don't we give your mom and Trevor some privacy."

Maddie laughed. "It's okay, Mom."

Trevor stooped to rub Misty's ears. The canine leaned into him, soaking up the affectionate pats. "How do you like the color, Amanda?"

Amanda's eyes lit up, and a huge smile split her face. "It's lovely! I still can't believe you two made me my own apartment. You didn't have to do that. But I'm so grateful."

"We wanted to, Mom." After nearly losing her mother, Maddie wanted to keep her whole family close. Building the apartment into their home allowed her mother to retain her independence and gave her, Trevor and the girls privacy, yet still kept them all close so they were never alone when they needed help or just wanted company.

An added bonus was that Piper and Paige got to see Grandma every day. She even ate dinner with them most days. And when both Trevor and Maddie had to work, nothing pleased Amanda more than watching her granddaughters.

"Oh, before I forget, the security company called me," Trevor said.

"Yeah? What did he want?"

"He wanted to check on everything. When I shut off the electricity to do some work, it sent them a notification. He wanted to make sure we were all right."

"I am so glad we decided to put in a full system," Maddie said. Even after her sister-in-law and Keith had gone to jail, she had still been plagued with nightmares. She woke up in the middle of the night to check on the twins to make sure they were still safe in their beds.

It would be a long time before she stopped doing that.

"I have to protect all my ladies," Trevor said. "Come see what we've completed while you were gone."

Holding hands, they strolled through the house to her mother's apartment. The dark blue walls and cream ceiling matched perfectly with the quilt her mother had made while showing the girls how to quilt. Maddie smiled to see that the cross-stitch patterns Paige and Piper had made for her birthday had been used to create pillows that were proudly displayed on the bed. Her mother had tried to show Maddie how to do needle work, but with her ADHD, Maddie had never had the patience or the ability to sit still long enough to finish a project.

From there, they moved to the twins' bedroom. Maddie mentioned her idea for painting the walls to them.

"I want my bed on a green wall!" Paige announced to no one's surprise.

"I want a pink wall," Piper added. "Can I have a pony painted on my wall?"

Trevor chuckled. "Let's do the color first. Then we'll talk about decorations."

Maddie knew right then there'd be a pony painted on the wall. She rolled her eyes. Her husband loved the girls like they were his own. Which reminded her...

"I do have a bit of news for all of you."

When she had everyone's attention, she continued. "I got a call while I was gone. Next week, we have our court date."

Paige and Piper stilled. "Does that mean Trevor will be our daddy, then?"

Trevor sank down, crouching so he was eye to eye with them. "Legally, yes. But you know you became my girls the day I married your mom. No piece of paper will make me feel more like your daddy than I do right now. To me, you are my daughters. Forever."

Maddie blinked her eyes to clear them. Was it any wonder she loved this man so much?

Paige threw her arms around Trevor's neck. "Then I'm going to call you Daddy now. Can I?"

He gently kissed her cheek. When he spoke, there was a rough edge to his voice. "I would love it if you called me Daddy."

Maddie waited to see how Piper would react. Although her younger daughter tended to be shy, in the past few months she'd grown bolder. Which meant she was no longer content to allow Paige to steal the show. Sure enough, within thirty seconds, Piper tugged on his arm.

"Yes, Piper?" Trevor's brown eyes sparkled with humor. Maddie saw the way he held his mouth rigid and knew he was holding in a laugh. He was very careful not to hurt their feelings.

Piper planted herself at his shoulder. "Daddy, I want a pony on my wall."

He blinked, then couldn't hold in his laugh any longer. Gathering both of them in his arms, he held them close. "We can do that. Especially since I know you're going to be seven in ten days."

Dinner that night felt like a celebration. Maddie almost told him her suspicions then. But she decided to wait and bide her time.

*

A week later, the family stood together in family court and listened as the judge approved the adoption. Paige and Piper Stone, formerly Blake, were now officially recognized as Trevor's children and shared his last name.

Amanda wept and hugged them all when the judge stepped down and left the courtroom. "Oh, I'm so happy."

He completely agreed with her sentiments but was afraid to speak at the moment. Actually, hearing that Paige and Piper were his struck a chord so deep inside him, his throat clogged with emotion. He settled for embracing them.

Finally, he cleared his throat. "News like this calls for ice cream."

"Yeah! Chocolate!" Paige announced.

"Cookie dough," Piper said.

Ushering them all out to Maddie's SUV, he drove them to celebrate with ice cream.

Later that night, both Trevor and Maddie went into the twins' room to tuck them in and say their evening prayers with them. Piper patted the large pony painted on her pink wall before climbing into her bed and pulling her covers up over her pony pajamas.

Paige had opted for butterflies on her green walls.

It amazed him how two people could look exactly alike but be so completely different. He looked forward to the years to come. God had truly blessed him. There was something especially sweet in hearing Maddie pray with them. She'd turned her back on God for so long, passionate in her rejection of Him. After her faith rekindled, he'd seen for himself that she was equally as passionate about serving Him.

They said good night and stepped out of the room, leaving a small night light on in the corner. Then hand in hand, they returned to the kitchen. Trevor emptied the dishwasher while Maddie made them both a fresh mug of decaf coffee. She added a splash of cream to hers. Trevor always drank his coffee black.

Once he tossed the dish towel in the basket inside the laundry room, he joined her on the sofa in the enclosed porch right off the kitchen area. She handed him his mug. He took a sip and set it on the table on his right side. Snuggling closer to his wife, he placed his left arm across her shoulders.

"It's been an eventful day." She tucked her head against his shoulder. These were the moments he lived for each day.

"It has," he agreed. "A great day."

He was a dad. Not a stepdad. He was a dad now. So much joy filled his heart, he felt ready to burst with it.

"We've been blessed."

"That's the truth." He reached out and snagged the handle on his mug to take another sip.

"Hey Trevor?"

"Hmm?" He swallowed the hot beverage and peered down into her hazel eyes.

"I was going to wait, but I decided today would be the perfect day to tell you…"

His breath caught in his throat. Shifting so he was sitting facing her, he searched her face. "Maddie?"

She grinned, her eyes sparkling with unshed tears. "I'm pregnant. We're going to have another child."

All the dreams he'd ever had coalesced into this one moment. There were no words to express the exultation surging through his veins.

Gently, he wound his arms around her and tugged her close. When their lips met, he let his kiss speak of his joy. His hope. His love.

Dear Reader

Dear Reader,

Thank you for reading Maddie and Trevor's story. It was a joy to visit LaMar Pond again so many years after I first wrote *Presumed Guilty*. I have always wanted to give Trevor Stone his own happy-ever-after story. I had to wait until I got the rights back to my first two books before I was able to make this dream a reality.

LaMar Pond and LaMar County are fictional places I created for my stories. With each story, they grew a little. I nestled them in my beloved rural northwestern Pennsylvania, so if you are from that area or passing through, you may see some familiar names. Why LaMar Pond? It was for my grandmother. By the time I was in high school, I only had one grandparent left. Two had died so long ago that I barely remembered them. My dad's mom, however, was a very real figure in my life and had a huge influence on me. When I wrote Presumed Guilty, I used her maiden name, LaMar, for my made-up town.

I hope you enjoyed this story. If you want to keep up with my writing updates, or learn more about my life, please sign up for my newsletter. I love to hear from readers!

Blessings,

Dana R. Lynn

Sneak Peak: Presumed Guilty

"There she is!"

"Melanie, can you give us a statement? How does it feel to be released? Do you still claim to be innocent?"

"She's a murderer! She should still be rotting in jail!" Prying questions, angry jeers and insults assailed Melanie's ears. She kept her head turned away from the mob standing behind the police officers stationed near the road. She had hoped the combination of the brisk March wind and the early hour would keep the vultures away. No such luck. Her heel slipped on a patch of black ice left over from winter. The ghost of a malicious chuckle reached her ear. She steadied herself, trembling.

A rock sailed through the air. It struck her pale cheek. She could feel blood well and drip down her face. She refused to brush it away, to allow them the satisfaction of seeing that she was hurt.

Wow. She was being stoned in public and no one seemed to care. If anything, the sight of her blood seemed to inflame them. The shouts grew louder, and someone started chanting, "Murderer! Murderer!" The crowd picked up the chant. It sent ice down Melanie's spine.

A muscled arm shot in front of her face, deflecting a second rock. The owner of the arm placed a strong hand on her shoulder. Not in comfort, but in an attempt to keep her moving. She didn't acknowledge him. She already knew that Lieutenant Jace Tucker agreed with the crowd.

"Officers, control those people!" he barked into the radio fastened to his shoulder.

Mel shuddered as Lieutenant Tucker's harsh voice washed over her.

Without warning, a swarm of hungry reporters closed in on her, threatening to swallow her whole. She ducked her head to avoid the cameras flashing around her. The cacophony of voices surrounding her was deafening, one voice melting into the next. At least the hooded sweatshirt she was wearing allowed her to hide part of her face. Hopefully, her bleeding cheek wouldn't make the evening news.

"Melanie, Senator Travis was quoted yesterday as saying you should have served more time for the death of Sylvie Walters. Any comment? Have you talked to his son, your fiancé?"

Ex-fiancé.

Not for the first time, Melanie struggled against bitterness towards the senator, who had used her court case as his own political platform to be harsh on crime. It wouldn't surprise her to find out he was responsible for this mob.

Melanie kept her face blank, but her chest tightened. One trembling hand slipped into her jeans pocket and closed around her inhaler. Please Lord, let me make it to the car.

One intrepid soul darted past her police escort and thrust a microphone into Mel's startled face. "Come on, Melanie. You were in prison for almost four years after being convicted of manslaughter. Surely there's something you'd like to say. A message for Sylvie's family, maybe?"

The callous remark slammed into her, robbing her of her breath.

"No comment, people. Give us room."

Against her will, Melanie glanced to her left to take in the man walking beside her. Lieutenant Tucker met her eyes briefly, his own as hard as flint, his face an inscrutable mask.

Why was he here? Couldn't they have found someone else for this duty—someone who wouldn't look at her with such clear disdain? Her knees trembled as he moved beside her. She resisted the urge to step away from him. Jerking her eyes forward, she strove to act as though he weren't there. But his image had been seared into her mind.

Strong. Determined. A man of faith. And the man who had personally slapped handcuffs on her and coldly recited her Miranda rights. And now she had to sedately walk by his side as if her heart weren't pounding and her insides quaking. Pull yourself together, Mel, she ordered herself sternly. All you have to do is make it to Aunt Sarah's house. Then you never have to set eyes on his odious face again. Okay, so maybe odious was a bit too strong a word. Still, she didn't think she would be too upset when he was out of her life for good.

She flicked a nervous glance at the stony-faced man beside her, shivering at the utter coldness in his deep blue eyes. His short blond hair was the color of wheat ripe for the harvest. His strong jaw was clenched as he walked by her side, emphasizing the distaste he felt for this assignment.

Well, that was too bad. She straightened her shoulders. Directly ahead, she could see the police cruiser waiting. All she needed to do was get through the gauntlet of reporters and angry protestors.

One of the protestors suddenly thrust himself forward. He planted himself in her way, ignoring the fierce scowl on Lieutenant Tucker's face. Stabbing a threatening finger at her, the demonstrator leaned in until he was almost touching her. Anger spilled from his eyes.

His pungent breath fanned her face. Mel stumbled back. Only the Lieutenant's iron grip on her arm kept her from falling. As soon as she had her balance, he released her. Fast. As if just touching her would contaminate him. Humiliated, she tried to walk around the man in front of her.

"You think you'll get away with this, don't you? Like father, like daughter." He sneered. "That poor girl's dead, and you go free after just a few measly years inside. But you'll never be free. We're watching you. We won't forget. You will pay the way you deserve, one way or another."

Melanie's stomach turned at the mention of her father and at the menace in the man's tone.

"Move along, mister, or you'll find yourself arrested for threatening her," Lieutenant Tucker ordered.

Not that he disagrees, Mel thought. Oh, she doubted the Lieutenant was the type to resort to vigilante justice, but it was clear he thought prison was exactly where she belonged. Despair welled up inside her. She clamped down on her emotions. No way was she going to show any hint of vulnerability. Not in front of these vultures. Her face a stoic mask, she let herself into the passenger side of the police cruiser. Her hands gripped together in her lap as she waited for Lieutenant Tucker to join her.

He slammed the driver's side door and started the car, muttering to himself. She waited until he had driven away from the crowd before taking her inhaler out and using it. She almost cried with relief as her inflamed air passages opened, allowing her to breathe freely. Lieutenant Tucker darted wary glances her way.

"Are you all right?" he asked her, his tone of voice suggesting he was only asking because he felt obligated to do so.

"I'm fine. Thank you for agreeing to drive me home."

He threw a furious scowl her way. "Yeah," he retorted, sarcasm heavy in his voice, "this is exactly what I wanted to be doing today."

"I'm sor——" She halted. No way would she apologize for any of this. Whether he believed it or not, she was the victim, and had been for a long time. Fueled by indignation, she found her anger and became bold. "Why are you even here? It's obvious you agree with those nuts out there."

His eyes widened, but were just as quickly shuttered.

Had she surprised him with her candor?

"It's my job. My boss felt you were in danger. Whether or not I agree, the chief wanted someone here. I drew the short straw. So here I am...a glorified babysitter for an ex-con."

That hurt. Melanie looked out the window as frustration clawed at her throat, making her voice tight when she spoke.

"I am not a criminal."

"A jury of your peers disagreed."

"I don't care." Her voice was low and husky. "I never sold drugs to anyone, especially not to teenagers."

He sighed and rolled his eyes. "Sure, sure. You were just a victim of circumstances."

"I was!"

"Look, lady..."

"My name is Melanie, not Lady."

"Whatever. The point is, Melanie, no matter how innocent you claim to be, all the evidence implicated you. I collected it myself."

"I know," Melanie responded bitterly. "But it was all circumstantial. What absolute proof was there?"

The lieutenant made a disgusted sound. "If you were so innocent, why the suicide attempt?"

Distress filled Melanie. An inarticulate sound of pain escaped from her throat, almost like that of a wounded animal. "I didn't...I wouldn't..." she choked out and turned to face the window. This time, the tears would not be held back. They trickled in a slow stream down her cheek.

She heard him sigh again but was determined to ignore him. Awful man. How dare he treat her this way? Even if she had been guilty, she had served her sentence and paid her debt to society. She knew in her heart, though, that she was not guilty. Proving it, however, had been beyond her power. Maybe if she could have remembered the night in question...she shook her head. She needed to move on.

"Melanie."

She refused to acknowledge him.

"Melanie, I'm sorry." The words sounded somewhat strangled.

She turned around from the window and glared at him. "Don't choke on your apology."

Unexpectedly, he chuckled. A shiver went down her spine at the pleasant sound. Under different circumstances, she might have been attracted to him. As it was, she couldn't help but view him as an adversary.

"I won't say that I don't think you're guilty, because I do." Melanie turned away from him. "I will apologize for my unprofessional behavior."

She nodded in acknowledgment. What else could she say?

The remainder of the thirty-minute drive from Erie to LaMar Pond was silent. Uncomfortable. Melanie kept her gaze fixed on the passing scenery outside her window. Only a few more minutes, she told herself when she saw the sign welcoming them to LaMar Pond. The car slowed as the lieutenant maneuvered past two Amish buggies. Lieutenant Tucker and Melanie both sighed in relief when her aunt's house came into view. It would have been humorous if the circumstances had been different.

Dear Aunt Sarah. Even with all the supposed "evidence," she had refused to believe her only niece could have committed the vile acts of which she was accused. Everyone else abandoned Mel. Her friends, her coworkers at the restaurant, even her fiancé. But not Aunt Sarah. For that alone, Melanie would be forever grateful.

The cruiser turned onto the gravel path that led up to the small cottage Sarah Swanson had built with her husband thirty years earlier. The area remained remarkably untouched in the years that followed. The closest neighbor was half a mile away. Melanie had always loved the peacefulness. The lack of people around appealed to her. Especially now. Impatience grabbed her. She tried to open her door. Locked. Throwing Lieutenant Tucker a scowl, she gestured toward the door. He rolled his eyes as he unlocked it. Ignoring him, she pushed the door open and ran up the front steps.

She stopped. Uneasiness shivered through her. The front door was open. Aunt Sarah never left doors open.

"What's the holdup?"

She whirled to face the grim-faced man stalking toward her.

"Lieutenant," she started. Stopped. If she shared her suspicions, he would think she was playing games. Her aunt had probably felt tired and left the door open so her niece wouldn't have to wait for her to maneuver through the house in her wheelchair. Mel remembered how drama wore her aunt out.

Melanie flattened her mouth into a determined line. Straightening her shoulders, she pushed the door open and entered. And screamed.

About the Author

Dana R. Lynn is an award winning author of romantic suspense and Amish romance who believes in the power of God to touch people through stories. Although she grew up in Illinois, she met her husband at a wedding in Pennsylvania and told her parents she had met her future husband. Nineteen months later, they were married. Today, they live in rural Pennsylvania and are entering the world of empty nesters. She is a teacher of the Deaf and Hard of Hearing by day and writes stories of romance and danger at night. She is represented by Tamela Hancock Murray with the Steve Laube Agency. Dana is an avid reader, loves cats and thinks chocolate should be a food group. Readers can contact her or sign up to receive her monthly newsletter at www.danarlynn.com.

Also By

Hidden Amish Target
Hunted at Christmas
Amish Witness to Murder
Protecting the Amish Child

Made in the USA
Monee, IL
14 February 2024